In loving memory of my parents and grandparents.

May they rest in peace knowing the example they have
set live long through my actions in life.

Chapter 1: Business meeting

Sean and Lee are on their daily duties. Collect money from all the shops under the protection of their organisation, the locally so-called Rising Skulls. Against a certain amount, the shop owners are guaranteed not to be robbed and the area stays safe for the customers. The recent social crises have raised tensions on the streets, and the opportunism of certain people makes sometimes a simple shopping session a trap for lonely persons.

The Rising Skulls jumped on the occasion to gain certain credibility towards the local community. Their apparent strong presence, their relatively good connection with local authorities and historical joy for illegal business is well known around. But because they never caused troubles to the actual community, the Skulls aren't pushed away. Their organisation is everywhere, but you can't tell from outside if somebody belongs to them as their only sign is to have a Skull tattoo with a Gothic letter 'S' on each side.

This morning, Sean and Lee are looking after Modern Street. Butcher, barber, and O'Donnelly's, the little pub. The routine makes it easy, smooth, and it looks like a well-oiled routine. Everybody know them, they know everybody. After grabbing their envelop, they finally leave the pub to reach out their car parked down the street. The noise of a police car gets louder and louder. Sean looks around but can't see any fight or on-going robbery. Just for the sake of habit, Lee puts a hand on his gun, ready. Suddenly, a car rushes from the cross-around, tyres are scratching on the floor and all goes fast. The car passes in front of them followed by the police car. The driver brakes urgently, makes a U-Turn, avoids the police car arriving full-speed behind him, and leaves through a small street. Within 15 seconds, that car just escaped from the police.

Finally getting into the car. On the way back, Sean can't stop thinking about that scene. It's fairly usual to see people being chased by the police, but to escape that easily is definitely surprising. At the depot, he goes straight to the manager's office:

- Boss, we need to talk, I may have some good news…

- What can I do for you, Secretary?

- You still look for a new driver to help us settling the transport business?

- Yes, if we have a driver, we can finalise the deal with the guys from Wexford and make a big money out of it… Why? Any candidate for the job?

While Sean goes through the story of this car escaping the police, Niall listens, quietly. That business would bring a fortune and make the Rising Skulls known in other counties.

-   Did you check his plate number?

- 10-D-14123 … Black. Nissan Qashqai I would say.

- Good work, Sean. Give this info to Aiden and track this guy down. It's worth checking on him and see what's he up to.

- I'm on it Niall.

As he walks out to the office, Lee goes straight to him to ask if that was about the car and what the whole story was about.

- Keep cool, kid, and focus on what you have to do.

- I don't want to lose my place here if somebody else is coming, you know

- There is no place to lose, and imagine something… If somebody new would join, you wouldn't be the most recent member; you would eventually stop doing all the shit for us. Alright?

- Ok, if you say so…

- Where is Aiden, kid?

- No clue, last time I saw him, it was yesterday night, and he was chasing a girl downtown.

- For Christ sake, he will never learn … Ok, go back to work, will track him down.

Then he tries his cell phone, no answer. Lighting up a cigarette, he tries again to call. Unsuccessful. He gets into one of the car of the organisation and decides to check at Aiden's house and see if he would eventually have crashed there after a rough night. Driving through the city, he sees few members at work, patrolling and accompanying people. Looks like nobody saw Aiden. Arriving at home, from outside Sean can hear loud rock music. Knocking the door, nobody comes to open the door. As the window from the living room is slight open, he decides to throw a rock to try and catch Aiden's attention. How big the surprise is when it's actually a girl showing at the window questioning the whole situation.

- He's taking a shower, he shouldn't be long anymore. Want some coffee?

- Who the fuck are you?

- I'm Aoife, I hang out with Aiden.

- Since when?

- Don't really know… So yae or nae on the coffee?

- Aye. Black, no sugar.

The lady ends up opening the door and goes straight to the kitchen to serve a coffee for Sean. Aiden turns out in the middle of the kitchen, just wearing a towel around him.

- Hey brother, what's up?

- What's up? Do you actually want to know what's up? You didn't turn up to fucking work this morning, we didn't have a clue where the fuck you were, you don't pick up your fucking phone, and I have fucking urgent job for you to do, that's coming from Niall.

- Alright, alright, I had a little night rush with … hmm … what's your name darling?

- (Sean responding) It's Aoife, you dumbass.

- How do you know? Darling, how does he know your name?

- Because at least, he paid enough attention to ask.

- Alright, you get out of my house. Sean, I get dressed and you bring me up to speed.

Sean drinks his coffee in the kitchen, smoking his cigarette and listening radio. Aiden pops up in the kitchen:

- So, what's the story, brother?

- We need you to track someone down, but that's a bit different than usual.

- Why should I track somebody down? Diarmuid is normally handling the Security stuff.

- You're our Road Captain, Aiden. The guy we need to search for isn't part of a gang, at least none I could recognise… I have a plate number, a model and an area I saw him … Do whatever you need to, Niall wants to talk to him. And quick, please.

- Alright will check what I can do.

Sean leaves the house, and Aiden starts packing his stuff. Cigarette, bills, lighter, sunglasses, gun. He drives through the city, not really knowing where and who look for. He stops in few pubs and shops to ask for any good information. Nobody seems to have any information. So he decides to stay around the area Sean and Lee would have seen him, maybe he would have any luck. The sun sets, still no sign of any black SUV. He decides to call for support, maybe somebody else could position himself at another place and help him on that:

- Hi Niall, it's Aiden. I try to track that dude for you… But so far didn't find any possible info on him, can you send me somebody?

- Look, we're all busy, I will check with Tom if he can send somebody over. He will let you know, alright?

The line cuts. Aiden knows nobody will come till the morning. The whole neighbourhood is very quiet and it's getting harder to stay awake. Slightly falling asleep, his phone rings:

- Yeah? What's up?

- Wake up, Aiden, it's Tom. All the guys are doing protection runs overnight, I will send you Ian and Liam on the morning, alright? Till then, don't dare sleeping we need that guy ASAP.

- Got it, tell the guys I'm in front of the butcher O'Connor.

- Will do. Good night.

Night is long and the traffic on that street is more and more quiet. Around 3am, listening political shows on the radio, a dark SUV approaches and parks about 100 meters ahead of Aiden. A guy gets off the car, then walks to an apartment block. Aiden watches this guy very carefully, and as he crosses the road, he looks nervously in all directions … 'There must be something about that guy, he doesn't seem relax enough to be innocent. He drives around to check on the plate number. 11-C-13311. Doesn't match with the plate that Sean noted down. But his behaviour still doesn't look normal. It's the correct car, the correct neighbourhood, the guy looks concerned. Would match enough to check further on him. He parks closer to that car and decides to follow him on the morning. Around 6:30, a car approaches Aiden's car,and stops next to him. Two guys get out, that's Liam and Ian, two members of the Skulls. They get into Aiden's car, while the other one leaves.

- What's the craic, Aiden? Why are we here exactly?

- Thanks for coming. We need to track down a random dude, he is driving a Nissan Qashqai, Niall wants to talk to him ASAP. He was seen escaping from police around here. You see that car over there? It's not the right plate number but a guy arrived in that car at 3am and looked weird and stressed. He might have changed the plates since that escape.

- Alright, what's the plan now?

- We wait till he leaves his flat; we follow him and see what's up to.

- Ok, I will go and grab us some coffee. Will be back shortly. Ian, you stay with Aiden.

As he walks out of the car and goes in direction to a shop, Ian starts playing with his phone and lights a cigarette.

- Not in the car, brother, get out if you want to smoke.

- Says the guy smoking two packs a day… Fuck that, I'm off.

Liam coming back to the car, sees Ian outside of the car smoking and looking pissed off.

- Don't tell me you got kicked of the car already?

- Not my fault, brother, I am not allowed to smoke in the car.

- Get in the car, kid, you will smoke later. Grab your coffee.

Both get into the car, start drinking their coffee in silence. People start to leave their houses one after the other but the car doesn't move. The street starts to get busy and traffic is piling up.

- If he gets out now, we are going to struggle to follow him without getting noticed.

- What if we go directly and ask him straight 'are you the police fucker?'

- Yeah, smooth, Ian, keep saying shit, you're in the right direction.

- We can't expose ourselves right on the street, interrogating somebody based on nothing. We are supposed to be there to protect people, you remember?

Time flies and around 8:45, finally somebody approaches the black SUV. The guy keeps looking around like when he arrived few hours before, and his eyes catch the Skulls car with the three guys inside looking at him. He stands there, starring at them, with strong look. He jumps into his car and drives straight onto the street. The Skulls know they got caught and they have anyway to talk to him at this stage. Aiden starts the engine and engage pursuit with the Qashqai. Aiden isn't the Road Captain of the Skulls by mistake; he knows all the streets, all the crossroads, all the shortcuts of the county. He used to be taxi driver before joining the organisation. As he gets closer and closer to the target, the Qashqai does the exact same trick to escape that he did with the police car. But this time, that's Aiden driving against him, so he gets trapped as Aiden brakes at same time and in same direction, so when the car makes a U-Turn, Aiden is right there blocking the road.

- Enough effort with this fucker, let's grab him and bring him back to the depot,

Liam pulls his gun out of his jacket and takes out the safety mode, ready to shoot.

- Get the fuck out of that car or I shoot you right in your head.

Nothing happens. Nobody moves. The engine is still running. Ian grabs his automatic gun and decides to get closer. Aiden knows that it's not going to show any positive sign to this guy having two guns in his direction.

- Guys, guns down. Right now.

As he moves towards the car, he puts his hands in the air.

- I have no gun, we don't want to hurt you or anything, we just want to talk to you. Really, man, it's
  all good, not to worry about us.

The driving-side window goes down.

- Who the fuck are you?

- We just want to talk to you. My name is Aiden, and
  the two little fuckers with me are Liam and Ian. We
  all work together for the same organisation, and
  our boss wants to talk to you.

- What the hell? Who's that? Why does he want to
  talk to me? I did nothing wrong with you or with
  anyone?

- Guys, go back in the car, let me handle this. Ok,
  mate, what's your name for a start?

- Aaron.

- Ok Aaron, let me approach to the car, I just want
  to talk to you, I will explain the whole story, alright.

- Aye. Come on.

- Ok mate. I'm Aiden, I'm the Road Captain of the
  Rising Skulls. Did you already hear about our organisation?

- Aye.

- Good. My boss Niall wants to talk to you because apparently you're pretty good at escaping from police.

- How do you know that?

- We look after this part of the city, and we make sure no shit happens here. Two of our men saw you doing your little drift trick to escape. Our boss needs good drivers right now and you don't look like you're any kind of rich kid, so you may want to listen his proposal...

- What kind of job does he have for me?

- That kind of detail I don't know, that's why it would be good for you to follow us to our depot so you can have a little chat with Niall.

- Well, I guess you won't leave me alone till I come with you, right? Let me call my boss and call out sick for the morning. I follow you.

- Good. And... Aaron, don't try to escape ever again. That shit doesn't work with me.

Aaron smiles. The whole scene is unreal. He actually can't believe what's going on. On their way to the Skulls depot, there was some tension in the car driven by Aiden... Arriving at the gate, Aiden slows down and park. Aaron parks next to him and goes straight to Aiden, with a closed face, looking all around him.

- Not to worry, you're in a safe place here. Follow me, I will bring you to the boss.

- Aye, bring me to the boss.

Going into the depot, Aaron knows he shouldn't make eye contact, he is in their house, not on the streets, nobody would know whatever would happen in here. He walks starring at Aiden's neck, which is straight ahead of him. From the corner of his eyes, Aaron distinguishes few people hanging around. Aiden stops in front of a black door, then turn back to Aaron:

- You go in there, I don't come with you.

- You serious? Why?

- I'm not your babysitter, kid, go on.

Aaron feels his palm sweating, his breathing is accelerating. He doesn't have a clue what he will find behind this door. He stands there knowing he can't go back anyway. Suddenly, the door opens. A guy stands there, smiling.

- Morning son, how are we? Please come in.

Aaron doesn't move, he actually can't. He is properly stunned by the behaviour of his host. He was expecting anything but a friendly person. As Niall shows him the way, he finishes by making two steps and get in the room.

- So, it seems you have few driving skills and you don't like the police patrols, is that right?

- Well… hmm … not sure how to answer that.

- Look, I'm not from the police, I guess you know that. The Rising Skulls are in this city for more than a decade now. Our main business is to ensure the security of the area, we escort people or shipments to make sure everything is going well around here. The social climate got fairly tense in the past years and we made sure we would protect our community from external and internal threats. But today, escort isn't making enough money. I have few other businesses, that keep us in green at the end of the month and allow me to pay my guys fairly above the standard salaries.

- Sounds mighty but .. What I am doing here?

- Why were you escaping from the police?

- Improper behavior on the road.

- I see your car outside, You changed the plate since yesterday, didn't you?

- Yes. I work in a garage, we have an old press to create plates, nothing easier than changing plates.

- And the car documents? You change them too?

- I'm fairly good with computers, I can do documents which look real enough to abuse police patrols for random checks.

- And if they check in their database?

- Then you see me escaping (he starts smiling more and more)

- How much do you earn at the garage?

- About 2200 net.

- Alright, here is the deal. I have a transport business to run, so far I have nobody of my crew able to do that, except Aiden but he's already too busy. I can double your salary in cash and make you participate in other deals to round up that number.

- What's this deal about?

- I won't tell you anything more till I know if you're in or out.

- I appreciate the offer, and your interest in me. But I have a girlfriend and I don't want to start illegal business because she wouldn't accept that. I'm struggling to close the months, that's for sure, but I can't afford to be involved in that kind of business.

- But why do you escape from police and change plates of your car? What's that all about then? Doesn't make sense to me.

- That's the adrenaline that makes me feel good. And I hate cops more than anybody on this planet, I love to see them struggling to follow me.

- Listen, son, think about it. We are well structured here, I can give you very good money for some fun work, and you wouldn't have to do anything else than what you like to do.

- Thanks for this meeting, I have to go now. (He stands, shake hands with Niall and walks out of the room)

- Hey Aaron! Think about my offer and let me know by tomorrow.

Aaron keeps walking without responding. On the way out, he feels so much more confident about the whole thing that he actually looks around at people, nobody even dare looking at him. His mind is just blown. What would make more sense to him; he can't even tell at that stage what he should do. 'Let's finish that day and talk with her about that, let's see what she thinks'.

At the garage the day seems never ending, the whole discussion turns in his mind and he can't stop thinking about the money, the job, and what would make more sense for his life. Surely his girlfriend Lisa would not like that idea of being involved in weird business. She never asked for much but Aaron wants to give her a better, more stable, less stressful life. 'Let's talk about it tonight, hopefully that will go well' he thought. Deep down he knows he should prepare himself for a big, big discussion.

Chapter 2: The Why and the What

19:30 on the dot. Closing time for the garage. As he gets back to his car, Aaron feels his heart beating harder and harder. It's time to go home. The keys into the flat door are making more noise, the echo of his shoes in the corridor is louder, his face is hard as steel.

Lisa walks out of the kitchen, smiling:

- Hey babe, how was your day? I will open a bottle of wine, I have great news!

- Tough day. Sounds good .. go on.

- You seem concerned, what's going on?

- Nothing… So tell me, great news, huh?

- Yeah, I will finally have my overtime paid off, should bring another 200 euros per month.

- What if I tell you you don't have to do overtime anymore and I can have twice my current salary just swapping jobs?

- You serious? That's unbelievable, what's that all about?

- I had a job proposal from the Rising Skulls to work for them; double salary and I can work as soon as I want.

- Rising Skulls? Are you kidding me? You're not a fucking outlaw, Aaron.

- Alright, love, look. We don't make enough money to move forward in life. We both know that. I want a house with proper isolation and hot shower anytime we want. I want two nice cars that don't need me to repair every other day like I have to for yours right now, I want to have other kids with you, that we can pay food and medicines, and we can take them on holidays like I never did with my parents because they were fucking broke.

- I want that too, but we do that legally or we don't do it at all. We are happy just like we are, we need to face reality, that ain't be good for us if you start to work for them.

- I can't pass on this opportunity to make big money… and it will be temporary, I will do that for few months, a year top, just to put some money aside and then go back to a garage.

- Aaron, listen to me carefully. You do that, I swear that you get out of the house straight away and you will never see me again. Is that clear enough? You don't take that job.

- Seriously? That's how you want to see things? I'm doing that for us, to give us a better life and a future.

- Ok, that's grand. Pack your shit and get out if you want to do that.

- You know what? I thought you would understand why I want to do that.

The way she looks at him now is new for Aaron. He never saw her looking so angry, disgusted, shocked. Deep down he feels the excitement of such a lifestyle, work with Rising Skulls was definitely something he would never have been expecting to have the opportunity. He is now standing at the entrance of the kitchen, starring at his girlfriend like she would change her mind. He knows her enough to know that's hopeless to expect anything. She seems so pissed that she doesn't even look at him. She is standing above the sink, like even looking at him would make her sick.

- I want to do that for us. For us, Lisa.

- Bullshit, we both know you always looked at them with admiration, I know you would fancy working for them.

- Give me a chance, just a chance, to show you that I can make it work. At the first sign of any kind of shit, I go back to the garage. For Christ sake, believe in me, I know what I am doing.

- Do you think it's that easy? That you can walk out of that kind of organisation whenever you want? In which world do you live?

- They came to get me, I can use that to set some conditions in the deal…

He sees in her eyes that she is slightly changing her mind set. Would there be any hope for her to agree on that move. She has that look, like a 5 years old kid which is afraid of changes, of the world outside. Aaron decides to walk slowly in her direction to see how she would react. She stares at him like at a wild animal. She seems scared. He knows how much she loves his smile. He just puts a big smile on his face, open his arms while getting closer, and just says quietly 'It's going to be fine, love, I will protect you' putting her head on his chest and kissing her forehead.

- I give you one chance, just one. Please don't disappoint me.

- I promise, love. I promise.

He feels her relaxing a bit in his arms, and knows he will need to be extremely careful in the coming days and weeks.

- I will talk to them tomorrow and check what they want me to do.

- Take care of yourself, baby, please. Don't do anything stupid.

- Aye, love. Don't worry for me. So, wine and dinner?

- Yeah, grab two bottles, after that conversation I'm going to need a whole lot.

Lisa is now smiling, and looks much more hopeful than she was at the beginning of the conversation. They both sit together and have a drink...

When the alarm rings on the morning, his stomach is stressed like it would rarely have been before. On his way to the depot, everything around him seems to be foggy. The noise of the cars sounds far away, the radio is off, and the people crossing the streets are shadows. As he doesn't know what to expect, how to behave in this world, he tries to think, to prepare himself, to establish a plan. He pulls his car on a street parking spot just in front of the entrance gate of the depot. As the gate is closed, he tries to find a bell to ring but can't find any. Looking around he notices a security camera, and few shots impacts on the walls. He hears somebody walking in his direction. The person stops, then the silence comes. Aaron just hears the man breathing on the other side of the door.

- Morning… hum… my name is Aaron, I was due to meet Niall today, do you know if he's there?

- Ok, wait here, I will check and come back.

The voice of that man just froze Aaron's blood. So deep, so cold, so strong. Very quietly, that man talks to somebody om the phone. 'I have here some Aaron dude for Niall. Should I let him in?'. A metallic click from the door, and a second one. The door opens, letting Aaron finally seeing that person. Short, tattoos, beard. Impossible to know if he would be in his thirties or forties.

- Hi there. Follow me, will bring you to him.

- What's your name?

- Who the fuck are you? The police?

Aaron is smiling though. He knows that this is part of the rough aspect of that kind of organisation. It will be hard to gain their respect, their tolerance, but once you get it, they will never take it back and get your back anytime you need them to.

Following this unknown guy through a not-so-well known place should be weird for him; he should feel insecure, unsure of his choice. But the excitement of the moment takes it all. The smell, the noise, all seems so good to him. A new world, a new start, and some sort of a dream coming true. Here we are. The guy asks him to wait in front of the office. His heart is beating so much that he feels his pulse in his head. Somebody opens the door. It's that guy again.

- Come here. Now.

As he gets into the office, he sees two men standing around Niall, sitting himself at his desk. Niall speaks straight to him:

- Aaron, thanks for coming. I don't present you to Aiden. That's Tom, the Operations Manager. So what's the story with you?

- I'm in. I can start immediately, just need to go to the garage and let them know. Does your offer is still on?

- Good. I'm actually surprised though that you didn't even ask more details about the job itself.

- I know I'm not going to bake cookies, Niall. The rest is up to you to fill me in.

- I will get the whole group approving your arrival, wait outside. Aiden, get the others in.

As he waits in front of the office, another door opens and a whole group of guys are now appearing. Aaron recognises Ian and Liam. They all stare at him with stone-cold look. Everybody walk into the office and the door shuts. What if they say No, and what if they say Yes. What would he say to the garage? Everything is going so fast and right now so slowly. He wants to know, he needs to know.

The doors reopen. He hears Niall's voice:

- Come in, Aaron.

Inside the office, everybody has the same closed up look.

- Welcome to the Rising Skulls, Aaron. You can be proud of it.

Aaron closes his eyes. He can't believe it, it's done. Half a second later when he reopens it, the whole scene changed. Niall is in front of him. The entire squad are smiling and punching table to celebrate his integration. Shaking hands with Niall.

- Let me present you to the whole team now. Tom, as Operations Manager, helps me to lead the business and the team. Aiden, the Road Captain, looks after planning our trips and that the whole business is carried in the best way. Here we have Sean, the Secretary. He handles the budget, the accountancy and the administrative piece of the organisation. Diarmuid is our Security Officer, he makes sure we take no risk and we are covering ourselves in our business and here in our offices. We have 4 members: Liam, Coilin, Ian and Lee. And now we have you as a Prospect. Any question so far?

- I will surely not remember all the names and funcions straight away, but will make my best. Thanks again to everybody, that's really cool, I will not disappoint you.

- Alright, thanks for that. Boys, the session is closed, you can leave. Aiden, Tom, you stay. Lee, shuts the door on your way out. So … Aaron… Tom will give you the ground rules of our organisation in a moment. First I need to tell you what you will do for us. Being prospect means you can't vote, you can't be part of decision-making. We can ask you pretty much whatever we want, whenever we want. You don't ask questions, you just do. Any problem with that?

- Understood.

- We have a new partner, they want us to carry their stuff from their warehouse up in Waterford to the Cork City and commutes. Every day you will go there, drop your car for loading, get back your keys and drive wherever they will ask you to. Never stop the car, never open the trunk, and never ask what you are actually loading. When they contacted me few weeks ago, I told them we couldn't handle their business because we were pretty maxed out already and I wouldn't have the capacity to do so. So what would be your main task, and when you're done with that, you come back here and we see if there is anything else you can do. Still no questions?

- Will I use my car or will I have a special one depending on what they ask me to carry?

- You have a Qashqai, right?

- Yes indeed, 2010.

- Should be okay, they just needed somebody with a SUV, so I guess that's alright.

- Fine, then no more questions for now.

- OK. So Aiden will help you with the traffic, the itineraries, what to avoid, what to go for.

- Fair enough, Niall. No problem.

- One thing matters to me. Loyalty. Make our business be fine, we will make sure you're fine too.

- You don't have to worry about that.

- All good then. Tom, he's all yours.

Tom stands up and walks out, followed by Aaron and Aiden. Aiden then splits to join the rest of the group while Tom takes another door. That's some sort of an old warehouse, it smells wet, there is dust everywhere and few cars are parked in one side of the place.

- You have all the garage basic tools over there if you need to do anything on one of our car. We put the car inside anytime; we don't want to take any risk.

- What kind of risk are you talking about?

- You will see, kid. So let's go back to the offices.

As they walk back inside the building, Aaron remains silent. So much to look around, so much to think about, and so much to remember. In the offices, they see Liam and Coilin leaving with backpacks. Aaron knows that as a prospect he shouldn't ask anything about the organisation and just do his piece, help the others and stay quiet. The visit of the building continues with the common room, with leather couches, a TV and few seats around a bar.

- That's where the lads chill between two jobs or whenever they want to stay over. It's pretty cool.

- Does anyone has a girlfriend or is married here?

- Most of us don't have any family, you know. This organisation is our family. Prove yourself here and you won't only make money but gain a whole new family.

- Sounds good...

- So we will give you a prepaid cell, you don't put any app on it, you don't give this number to anyone. You always answer your phone, 24/7, we don't care if you are banging a girl or taking a nap. We will check your car to make sure you don't have any electronic system on it that could locate you. All good for you? You don't seem to have many questions… Are you just slow and you don't get what I say or are you just very motivated and will just take it as it comes?

- Despite the fact my parents always laughed at me saying I was slow, they were kidding, so I guess the second option is the right one.

- Alright. Go to your garage, grab your shit and give your resignation. When you will be coming back, we will go and meet our new partner to present you to them.

- Ok, will make it quick. For how long will I be prospect?

- Normal process is up to a year, but it depends as well on how you serve the group. Now move, we will be waiting for you here.

- Aye, boss.

As he walks back to his car, Aaron can't help himself but smile. As hard as he tried not to smile too much in front of

Tom not to look like an idiot, the pressure becomes now too hard. Sitting on his car, engine turned on, he looks at Tom and the rest of the crew going back to their occupation. It's time to go to his garage, quit his current job and make that big step in his life. As he drives through the city, he remembers he has no valid reason to give to is employer to leave out of a sudden. 'Let's improvise, anyway, wouldn't be the first time', he thinks.

Lost in his thoughts as he is driving, he sees a police car overlapping him very fast and starts horns and lights. He pulls the car over, turns the engine off and waits, calm and silent. The police officers get out of the car, one stands in front of the car while the second one approaches Aaron's window.

- Do you know why we stopped you, sir?

- Unfortunately no idea, officer.

- You kidding, right? The red light you just drove through?

- Wait, no, it can't be, it was green!

- We were driving just behind you, I'm sure it's recorded on the camera we have on board.

- Oh really? Look, I'm sincerely sorry for that, I was going to work and I was maybe lost in my thoughts, I know I have to focus on the road for the safety of others though.

- Alright, listen, kid. You seem genuine, I will write you a protocol for a simple improper driving, you won't lose any point on your license but we will keep you in mind, next time we catch you for anything, I will make sure you pay for it. Understood?

- No problem, officer, thanks a million, that's very kind of you.

He doesn't know how he feels anymore, he sees in slow motion. That's the adrenaline, he feels his blood running through his body like wild horses in the valleys. Everything is going so fast around him. The cars passing by, the people on the street. He takes a deep breathe, turns the engine on and leaves the place to finally go to the garage. As he parks on the side of the garage, his boss walks out of the building towards him. He has a black trash bag in his hands. His face is closed, his look is dark. As he throws the bag in Aaron's arms, his mouth finally opens. 'I know what you're here for. They called me. I packed your shit for you, get out of my business and never come back. I really thought you could be someone good. I believed in you. I treated you like my son. You better get going A.S.A.P'. He turns back and leaves. Aaron is standing there, holding the bag. He doesn't move, he doesn't breathe. His heart hurts. He knows that there is no coming back from this point.

Jumping in his car, he heads then back to the Rising Skulls headquarters. A whole chapter of his life just closed. Actually, that's a whole new life beginning right now. New rules, new game. Hence a new player.

Opening the clubhouse door, Diarmuid is standing there, alone. He looks deeply at Aaron, his eyes aren't blinking, his breathe is silent, his mouth is closed. 'Let's go, kid, we all wait for you'. Diarmuid, opens the meeting room door. The whole organisation is sitting at the boardroom table, Niall leading the table. Everybody looks at him, he feels his heart beating so hard in his chest. Tom stands up, grabs something black in a plastic bag at his feet and walks towards Aaron. 'Welcome to the Rising Skulls, Prospect. The ground rules are simple. You can assist to the meetings only when we allow you to, you don't wear any patch on your hoodies except the Prospect one. Only full members are allowed to have the Skulls symbol. Now put your hoodies on and go to the warehouse, our cars need a lot of repairs. I dropped a list of tasks to do for you on the desk.'

As he walks to the warehouse, putting his hoodies on, he looks at the 'Prospect' patch on the top of the right sleeve. It's getting more and more real. Arriving in the warehouse, he can't avoid having a look at all the cars parked and waiting for him. His curiosity makes him imagine whatever has been done with these cars, illegal activities, weapons, money, people. All the cars are there, parked randomly. Aaron looks at the desk, full of cartons, tools, objects. On the wall, a board with the list of all repairs to be done and phone numbers of places to get spare parts and tyres. 'That's a fucking long list… Better start now' thinks Aaron. He takes out his hoodies, his bracelets, his watch, and starts by Niall's car. A nice dark blue BMW, leather seats and full of options. He turns on the radio and starts working. As he goes from one car to another fixing, modifying, checking, few members come and go, they don't look at him or throw some words. Aaron knows that his first weeks and months will be tough, as everybody will be checking his character and capacity to actually fit in this environment. The time flies, it's already late afternoon, Aaron didn't even think about taking a lunch break as he wants to finish his duties as fast as possible. It's almost 7pm when the warehouse door leading to the office opens. A strong voice screams: 'Prospect, get in here'.

Aaron drops everything he has in hands and runs through the stairs. Ian is in the reception lobby. 'Niall is waiting for you, hurry up'.

- Are you done?

- I have several of them done at this stage, and still need.

- I don't want to know, the question was simple enough, are you done?

- No, I'm not.

- Ok, then what are you waiting for? Go back and hurry up.

Niall's eyes were cold as ice, and his breathe, very quiet, and isn't really helping Aaron to feel good. Running back to the warehouse, he gets back to work trying to sort priorities and what can be done the quickest possible so most of cars would be ready to be used. While he starts changing tyres on Ian's car, his phone rings. Looking at the screen, that's Lisa's name displayed. He lets the voicemail get the call. Twice. Then third time. At the fourth call unanswered, he finally decides to write a text claiming 'Can't talk right now, busy at work'. He doesn't have the time to drop back the phone on the phone that Lisa answers 'No problem, take care, love you'. Not bothering answering, he goes back to the car. The crew starts to come over, grab their keys and leave the place to go home. Meanwhile Aaron, all alone in the large warehouse, keeps working on the cars. It's only 4:30 when he finishes. Looking at his mobile phone, he sees 7 missed calls, four messages and the tone of each of them is escalating more and more. As the guys will be back only few hours later, so better stay on site and have few hours of sleep.

He switches off the radio, the lights, grabs all the keys and walks upstairs to finally crash on the couch, still dressed, still dirty.

Chapter 3: The Test

7:34. That's the time displayed on his mobile screen when Sean and Liam throw a glass of water on Aaron's face.

- Wake up, prospect, it's time to see what you're capable of, screams Sean.

- For fuck sake, guys, that wasn't necessary, Aaron responding and moaning.

- Jesus, when was the last time you took a shower, kid? , is asking Liam. You smell like my grandmother.

- I rather don't want to know the reason behind that. Will hit the shower now, will be ready in 10 minutes.

- You better be taking two minutes or you're out of here, quietly says Liam.

While Aaron runs to the bathroom to get ready, Tom enters the clubhouse.

- Is that me or all the cars are ready to go?

- Ask the prospect, he's in the shower, responds Sean.

- Prospeeeeeeect, screams Tom, get in here.

Strange sounds come out of the bathroom and suddenly Aaron runs out of it, just wearing underwear and still being completely soaking wet.

- Yeah, what's the problem?

- Well, first, you're fucking wet and wearing undies while talking to me. Fuck that. Second, are all our cars ready to go now?

- Yes, all done except Aiden's tyres, out of stock, should be delivered this afternoon, will get this done as soon as he's back.

- You better be dry and dressed, that's going to be a busy day for you.

- Aye, will come back in a sec.

Running back to the bathroom, he comes back wearing the same time dirty shirt and pants than the day before.

- Ok, says Diarmuid. For a start, you can't keep the same clothes than yesterday. You fucking stink, you look like shit. So once we tell you what you will have to do, go back home, change and start your mission then.

- You will drive to the address given to you by Aiden, continues Tom. You will present the vehicle, they will expect you, and we will give them your registration number. You let the car to theiwarehouse guys, they will lock you in a room with coffee and you will wait till they call you back.

- This is one of our biggest potential new customers. Don't mess it up. They wanted a good driver that can escape from cops and special situations, so hopefully you'll be their guy, follow Diarmuid. Under no circumstances, you open the trunk or ask them anything. They will give you the delivery address and same process when you deliver. They will expect you, put you aside and give you back the keys whenever they are done.

- And then what, should I come back here? Asks Aaron.

- Once you get back your keys, drive away and stop somewhere, call Diarmuid and you will get new instructions, explains Tom.

- Sounds like a plan; I'll go home and then drive there.

Grabbing the sticky note including the addresses of collection and delivery, the whole plan was flying in his mind. No time to waste, he jumps in his car and drives to his home.

That's only on his way back, stopped at a traffic light that he thinks about seeing his girlfriend and their kid. He was so much focused on his work that he forgot all of his 'normal' life for a moment. Parking just in front of his apartment block, he looks up to the building, breathes deeply and walk through the door. Going into the apartment, he can't help but notice how quiet the place is. No toy or anything else is on the floor or misplaced. Lights are off and windows are closed. Aaron walks into the bedroom, swaps tee-shirt and jeans, then swiftly go to the bathroom. He exits the bathroom with a bag containing the very basic stuffs, back to his bedroom. He throws few shirts in a backpack and rushes out of the apartment. On his way down the stairs, he hears something opening the mailbox, and in the meantime a kid talking very quietly. That's his son's voice; he could recognise it in the middle of a storm. As calm as possible, arriving at the ground floor, he finds Lisa grabbing Luke by the end and ready to walk through the stairs. The kid just jumps in his father's arms:

- You could have called, I was worried! Where have you been since yesterday?

- I'm sorry, love, I was working till the middle of the night, they test my capacity to follow the orders.

- Which orders? What testing? What happened now?

- You don't have to worry, everything is going fine. I will surely have a bit of a hectic schedule for the first weeks but I see them, they all now and they have actually a quiet life.

- I don't give a shit, you should let me know when you don't come back home. I was scared to death!

- Okay, I get it, I'm sorry. Look, I have to go now, I am in a mission, will write to you later, alright?

- If you want to be alive, you better!

She was half-smiling now that she heard his voice and saw him, and he notices it. Kissing both kid and girlfriend on the forehead, he grabs his bag and walks out on the street. Looking at the address, Aaron understands that this must be somewhere totally isolated in an industrial area. In the car, he checks that there is nothing especially visible in his car that could catch the attention of people loading/unloading the car.

Kilometers go flying and he is almost there. He's now in the correct street, needs to find the right spot. Arriving in front of the building number 33, Aaron thinks 'not complicated to recognise, this is better guarded than the White House'. Tall, strong men watching the main entrance, and now starring at Aaron's car. After few seconds, one of the security guy walks towards the car. His sunglasses are very dark, it doesn't help Aaron to feel any cooler:

- What's your name, kid?

- Aaron. I'm here to drop my car.

- I know what you are here for. We will let you in, stop straight after the gate, let the engine on and get out of the car, we will show you where you will have to wait.

- Ok.

As the security guy waves at the other one to open the gate, Aaron feels like he is getting more and more nervous. He drives slowly through and stops the car right after the gate. Engine still on, he quietly opens the door, steps out and look around. The warehouse, from the road, looks like in a disastrous shape. But once you see through the gates, this is clearly a high-running factory of some sort. One of the guard grabs him by a shoulder and literally throws him into an open door of the building:

- You get fresh coffee, chocolate bars, and a chair, stay inside till we tell you something else.

- Ok, how long does it take, you reckon?

- You're not here to ask question, you're here to drive.

No time for Aaron to say anything, the guard is walking away and slams the door. Enjoying the complimentary stuff, scrolling on his phone, only after 25 minutes the door opens again and the same guard shows up:

- It's ready, time to move.

Dropping everything to stand up, Aaron feels his curiosity has never been that high in his entire life. Looking at his car from about 30 feet, it looks absolutely normal. From 20 feet as well. And still the same from 10. The guard gives him the keys and says:

- I will show you the delivery address; you can't have the paper, in case you get pulled by the police. If that's the case, you don't say anything, you don't say where you got the car, where did you load the stuff, and where. Understood, kid?

- Doesn't sound too complicated for now. Anything I need to know about the car itself?

- Don't try to open the trunk. Don't try to look through the back seats. We installed sensors which will send us a message if you try to open the trunk or the back seats. At destination they have a box which deactivates it with a unique code that we will give them once you depart from here.

- Ok, show me the address and I'll fuck off.

- Here, have a look, take your time.

Aaron reads the sticky note few times, doesn't sound complicated so decides to leave straight away. The guard approaches back and says:

- By the way, we got detectors all over the car. I would be you, I wouldn't try anything stupid.

- That wasn't my attention.

- Good luck kid.

Leaving the premises, Aaron gets into the main road few minutes later. The destination is about 35 minutes' drive away from there. Reaching then the highway, he feels like he's randomly driving around and he's not really part of anything illegal. A casual week-end afternoon. Going through the South Ring, he goes around the city very smoothly and the traffic is almost none. Going into the country side roads now, with approximatively 10 kilometres to go. Everything seems to be so quiet, Arctic Monkeys in the CD player, rocking sunglasses and enjoying coffee. Going through a small town, Aaron can't help himself but notice that a grey SUV started in some sort of hurry and remains at a fair distance of him when he leaves the town. 'Must be some paranoia, that's ok'. As the road gets straight the SUV suddenly speeds up, overlaps brutally Aaron and gets in front of him. It doesn't take a second to Aaron to understand what's happening, and that he needs now to find a way to get him and his car out of that situation. No time to think, there needs to be some action taken straight away. The SUV starts slowing down more and more to avoid causing an accident and have Aaron immobilised. Time to do something, thinks Aaron. He stops completely, surprising the other vehicle. Then starts faking making a U-turn. The other vehicle is now making a proper U-turn while Aaron fakes struggling to perform it. When the SUV starts driving towards Aaron, he turns into the opposite direction and goes just aside of the SUV to keep driving in the original direction. He goes now as fast as possible, on roads that he never drove on, having his heart now literally out of his chest with so much excitement. He doesn't even know where he needs to drive to, the planned destination isn't really an option, the clubhouse either, and the SUV is still driving behind him and not losing any distance. Everything around him seems more and more blurred. The car is literally at its limit on every curve of the road. Aaron is now so focused on going fast and avoiding leaving the road that he doesn't look in the mirrors to see where is the SUV. After an epic minute which seems to last an hour, he finally take a look and doesn't see the car behind him anymore. 'Let's keep going, must have been freaking out on the road', thinks Aaron. As he slows down to a more legitimate speed, he feels his heart beating to a less legitimate one. That adrenaline, that speed, that sense of urgency in every move he made. 'Soon enough I'll be there'. As he gets into the industrial area, he slows down to start reading the signs and indications that could help him to locate the warehouse. All the walls are grey, all the doors are rusty and the dust flies behind him as he drives on a dirty track. 'Here we go, finally, Jesus Christ'. No security guard, no light visible through the windows, the gate firmly closed. Aaron opens the door, steps out and starts walking towards the gate. No one seems to be around. He starts thinking about the address, he looked at it, and he knows he's at the right place. Knocking at the gate. Nothing. Not any kind of sign of human presence. He starts walking around the corner, in case there would be another gate to get in. Minutes are passing by, when he comes back to the car. Aaron hears a ringtone, somewhere around him. He then tries to focus on where it is coming from. Moving in all directions, the wind not helping, he finally gets closer. The sound seems to come from under a sort of wooden piece. The ringtone stops. Aaron grabs the wooden piece and takes it out, then takes the phone slowly in his hands like it would explode by moving it too quickly. On the screen, he can see a missed call notification, indicating that it was from a Private number. He can't stop starring at the phone. Who dropped it here, why it was left just next to the entrance gate of an abandoned site, is this someone trying to reach him out for anything? He doesn't have the time to think further than the phone rings again:

-   Hello? , says Aaron

-   Are you the delivery man?

-   Whom am I talking to?

-   The guy paying Niall to do a job.

That's at that time Aaron knew it was the right person and not a trap. Mentioning Niall was definitely a proof for him that it was okay to talk about his job.

- Yes, I arrived at the address that was given to me. Site looks closed.

- Don't worry for that. Just stand in front of the gate, someone will come out of the warehouse.

- Aye, will wait in front.

As Aaron hangs up, he puts the phone on the front of the car and walks to the gate. Looking frenetically for any sign of life around the warehouse, he desperately doesn't notice anything. Suddenly, two cars are rushing around him and braking violently to stop on each side of him. He has been so focused on looking at the building than he didn't hear them arriving. Several men jumping from each car are now surrounding Aaron, pointing guns at him. One of them, unarmed, walks towards him:

- I guess you're Aaron. Not much of a truck driver look on you, I must say. You'll come with us. And you give your car keys to one of my guys.

- I've been told to deliver this to the warehouse, not on the street. So except if you let me get in, which will prove you're actually the consignee of this shipment, I will nicely get back in car and fuck off home.

The smile on Aaron's face is full of arrogance as far as the men facing him were concerned. Deep down, his heart was about to stop due to a panic attack.

- You've some balls, son, and no doubt about that. You have six guns pointed at you and you think you have a choice here.

- Till I delivered that car as planned, I am responsible for it, so I don't see why I should care about your guns.

Aaron's eyes are darker than ever, he tries to look as serious and sure about himself as possible. The main man, which started the conversation, is now staring at him without a word, waiting for any action or move. All the other men are standing there. The awkward silence reigning now doesn't help Aaron to feel more secure.

The main man starts walking towards him now:

- You either die now and we grab the keys ourselves or you give them to us and you stay alive.

- Well, then you may ask to your bodyguards to pull the trigger cause I am not going to give you anything.

- Ok, as you wish, continues the guy now looking over his shoulders to his crew. Get him, now!

Aaron is petrified, as he sees most of the crew rushing towards him. He trows a desperate punch into the first coming to him, but soon feels like a rock hitting his stomach, then another one in his ribs. He falls on his knees. The whole crew facing him are quickly tying his hands and his feet.

- Drop this asshole in the trunk, we wasted enough time. Frankie, you drive his car.

Carried like a potato bag into the first car's trunk, Aaron still feels the punch he received into his ribs. All gets dark as a man closes the trunk, and then Aaron feels the car starting to drive. He tries to listen to the discussion in the car:

- You know where we go? Says a first voice.

- No idea, let's follow Frankie, says a second one.

- Can't believe what we are doing now.

- Doesn't matter, it has to be done; you know how precious this business could become for the Skulls in Cork. We need to support that.

This last sentence is confusions suddenly Aaron's minds. Why these people are trying to support the Skulls of Cork if they are stealing the first shipment for an important business. And surely not supporting anyone by kidnapping their prospect. He can feel now that the car slows down, and the road gets more and more bumpy. He lost track of time and location. The car finally stops and doors open. Trunk still closed and he doesn't hear any sound around him. 'Another magical day to be alive', thinks Aaron, ironically. Few minutes later, which seemed hours for him, he hears a deep voice approach the car. The trunk finally opens and the light hits Aaron's eyes blinding him. After few seconds, trying to open his eyes, the only thing he can see is a fist punching him straight into his chest. And God knows how much that hurts. Looking at Aaron absolutely suffocating and still in the trunk of the car, the 'man with the deep voice' says to the responsible of the punch:

- What kind of weird stuff did you mother do to you to make you so stupid? I told you to weaken him, not to cause a heart attack.

- I don't know, it just happened, sorry boss!

- Joe and Stephen; carry him inside and drop him on the table. Attach his hands and feet to the table feet.

Still suffocating, still half-blinded by the light, Aaron can't resist to the hands pulling him out of the trunk. Like a dead body, he's dropped with as much care as a butcher carries his pieces of meat. He slowly catches his breath when the entire crew that met him at the entrance of the warehouse finally gets into the room. They all have black hoodies this time:

- Is that already my birthday or some shit? Engages Aaron. Cause let me tell you, I do like bondage, but usually I'm the dominant.

- We will break each bone of your body, then let you bleed, till you tell us who sent you, what's in your car and where did you load that stuff?

- You know my name so you know who sends me. For the rest, I think it's time to call my lawyer.

- Shut up now, enough jokes for today. So you still have anything to say, right?

- No-fucking-thing to declare. Like in the airport cust…

Aaron doesn't have the time to finish his sentence that he feels like a hammer on his stomach. And here comes back the suffocation.

- So, you idiot, continues the deep voiced man, We are listening.

The prospect tries to talk but no sound comes out of his mouth.

- I guess if you don't say anything, we can continue. To beat the shit out of you. Joe, enjoy.

Few punches later, surprisingly enough, Aaron doesn't feel any better.

- So, Aaron, before I completely lose my shit and shoot a bullet in your head, how about you tell me something…

- If you don't pull the trigger and I talk, my boss will do it himself, so either today or tomorrow I'm dead.

- Oh, wonderful, you got it. Finally we have someone that understands how things will go either way.

- So, how about we get this over and you make my skull look like a strainer?

The deep-voiced man, walking around the table, stops just next to Aaron's head. He grabs his gun, takes out the safety, and puts it between the prospect's eyes.

- That's now or never, son. What's your final word?

- Kiss my ass, man, I won't talk. Pull the trigger and have a nice day.

- Joe, go get them, he's ready.

The deep-voiced man drops his gun next to Aaron's face, gets his knife and starts cutting the ropes holding the hands and feet.

- What the hell is going on here? Screams Aaron.

- You will soon find out, son. Hang in here for a minute.

Before there is a chance to ask any question, the prospect sees several persons entering the room. And all the faces familiar. Niall, Tom, Aiden, Diarmuid, Liam and Ian are there.

- How did the kid behave, Jerry? Asks Niall to the deep-voiced man, which has finally a name.

- Didn't say shit, smart enough to understand what was coming and what would be the consequence of opening his mouth. And made few jokes to entertain us.

- I see, continues Niall now looking to Aaron after shaking hands with Jerry. So, kid, here is the story, we had to test you and see if you would rat or release any information. See where you are about the whole confidential side of the business and if we could rely on you to the point you would rather die than give any information.

- You got to be kidding, and what about all the shitty treatment I got? That wasn't necessary! Screams Aaron now trying to get down from the table.

- I present you our Nomad crew, they are our Special force equivalent, and we call them for sensitive missions like that. They are surely not angels or sweet hearted. Our customer was asking us to do that little trial as we told him we needed to recruit a special kind of person for this new business.

- Lovely, are we done for today or was that only foreplays? Says Aaron looking back at all the Nomad crew standing in a corner.

- Enough jokes for today, prospect, grab your keys and drive back to the clubhouse, we will catch up later with you.

As the prospect tries to walk out, with most of his body hurting, Aiden walks towards Aaron, smiles and grabs him in his arms:

- I'm proud of you.

- Thanks, brother, responds Aaron.

He then finally makes his way out after getting his keys back from the Nomads. On the way back to the clubhouse, he can't help himself but laugh… The Road Captain of the Rising Skulls proud of him means something for him; that matters and tells him that he's in the right way, doing the right thing.

He gets into the bathroom as soon as he's arrived and starts undressing to hit the shower. In the mirror, he sees all the traces of hits he received. Blue, green, purple, whatever color you can think of, he has them on his body. Covering them with his hand, he can't stop thinking about what a crazy day it was, but as well how positive it ended for him.

In the meantime, still in the Nomad clubhouse, Niall and Jerry are discussing face-to-face, drinking whiskey:

- Listen, Niall, my charter gets busier every month, we have new businesses everywhere that may be good if you let us know for anyone valuable that could help us on some missions. Today we were in Cork, tomorrow we must help the Sligo chapter, by the end of the week we have a raid to do as well in Waterford.

- I may have an idea, but I need to bring this back to my charter, vote and see what the result is.

- I guess if you recruited the new one is because you are already tight in resources?

- No, that's more because no one else aside Aiden would be able to cover that kind of mission and he's already very busy coordinating and support-ing all our activities. And the members, they may not have the required skills for that, you know…

- So what are you thinking to help me out?

- My plan, Jerry, is to propose to allocate Diarmuid and one of the member to the Nomads for the time being, might be part time or full time based on our business here in County Cork. Maybe Ceilin with Diarmuid, they are getting along very well.

- The Security officer? You would give us one of your officers? I can only tell you how surprised I am…

- Most of the guys in my organisation wanted to be in that role few years ago when I assembled the crew. I am curious to see who would step in.

- Watch that new kid, he might be useful to you in the future…

- Time to go home, Jerry, thanks for the help today, and don't worry, brother, we will sort you out temporarily.

- Thanks, brother, appreciate that. Take care of yourself.

Chapter 4: Thirty-eight minutes Chrono

That's 3 weeks now that Aaron did his first shipment, and it's becoming his daily business. He is getting recognition and appreciation from the Rising Skulls and from the customers too. He's now serving three different runs throughout the days, without getting noticed by the police.

Things changed a bit within the Skulls. Finally it's Liam which went out to the Nomads group with Diarmuid. They come back a day each week to grab some stuff and deal with local obligations. Aiden took over the Security Officer role on top of being Road Captain, which makes him very busy and stretched between all his duties. Sean remains Secretary and Ceilin, Ian and Lee kept their Member status. Aaron works now exclusively for Aiden, and is supported in the garage by two other hang-arounds. They aren't part of the organisation but come over after work to get few hundred euros.

Everyone got a little bit nervous when Diarmuid and Liam were transferred. The first one kept his Security Officer status within the Nomads. The second one has been assigned to the daily duties and helping anyone that would need to.

Niall had to involve Tom much more on the day-to-day duties to fill in the gap, which didn't make this last one very happy. Tom spent half of his life in this organisation already and fought hard to be in that position. Going back to daily business feels to him like a downgrade in his situation. He always wanted to be one day taking Niall's place whenever he would retire.

More Aaron spends time with the crew and more he believes that's where he belongs and he can see now a real outcome of his involvement. Money is now flowing as he gets two to three times more money than in his previous job. All the money brought back home is directly going to Lisa's hands to pay everything for her and Luke. He doesn't go home much, few times a week to drop the money and catch up with both of them. On a Tuesday evening, as he puts Luke into bed, Lisa is waiting for him on the couch to talk:

- Do you know that your son is asking 'Where's daddy' approximatively ten times a day?

- I know, love, believe me that is no fun for me not to see you both, but we both know where our life was going.

- I know times were tough but look at us now, we don't see each other, and we get more and more distant...

- Look, if I wouldn't have been going there, you would have worked more as well so we wouldn't have been seeing each other much! Now I took my responsibilities and bring enough money back home so my wife and my son can have food in their plates and have clothes on their back.

- I know, and I love you for taking care of us like you do, but could you discuss with them to have a bit more free time?

- We are all very busy, and you know I told you that we sent two guys to support another charter. That's why as well I make more money than planned, because I work more than I should. I hope it's going to be better whenever they come back to Cork.

- Do you believe what you say?

- I have to. I have to hope, that's the only thing to keep me going. I want to see my kid grow up, I want to see my wife. For now, I will see the money, pay our debts and hope for a smooth life once we are back to a decent financial level... Ok, got to go, will have an early start tomorrow, will try to come by as soon as possible.

- Please write me at least once a day to tell me that you're fine... I'm worried, you know that.

- I promise, love.

Kissing her on the forehead, then walking out, Aaron knows that his family needs him as much as he needs it. See his wife worrying is an image that bounces in his head the whole night. On the morning, as he goes onto the garage to start working on vehicles, Niall shouts his name through the stairs:

- Aaron, come here, now!

Running through the stairs, he already starts responding:

- What can I do for you?

- Why aren't you yet on your way for your first run?

- I just wanted to finish one or two vehicles before leaving, that won't take long. And I found new shortcuts on the way, very secure and saving 5 minutes approximatively.

- Sounds very good, I see you master your business already. Everything still goes as you thought joining us?

- Yes, sure, in my previous job I was leading few mechanics, and I do that here too, so that's fine. Maybe one day I will be entitled to more responsibilities and have my own back tattoo.

- Back tattoos are for officers, and you know that to become officer, it takes time. It needs patience and lots of efforts and sacrifices.

- And you know already patience isn't my biggest strength, boss. I'll prove you that I can become an officer. I could be your right arm and we both know that you need one.

Without leaving any time to Niall to respond, Aaron turns around and walks away, back to the garage to finish his work. As he looks at the kid walking away, Niall can't stop smiling at how self-confident Aaron his.

Back to the garage, Aaron quickly finishes his car, gives instructions to the hang-around staff helping him, and then leaves for the first run's collection point. Arriving on site, he drops his keys and goes into the waiting room. As he walks out few minutes to smoke a cigarette. One of the guard walks directly towards him:

- Go back inside; if my boss sees you outside, he will kill me.

- Don't worry, stay with me, you will see I don't even look inside the building. Here, do you want a cigarette?

- Yes, sure, let's hope for that.

As they start talking together, the guard feels more and more confident and comfortable with Aaron being around and releases some information that could be helpful to the Skulls, like knowing there are other businesses like this one, and currently being taken care of, who is handling security runs for these. Aaron remains quiet and listens. Few minutes later, the other guard drives Aaron's car out of the warehouse and let the engine runs while he swaps his place with the prospect.

Aaron leaves the yard, and the two guards now talking together:

- What were you talking about together?

- Nothing, you know, just chatting.

- You better be only chatting, I remind you that we are not supposed to be talking with external people.

Every time Aaron drives, he has few GPS systems running to show the best itinerary and avoid police controls. Always trying to improve the time and the mileage without putting his cargo at risk.

Aiden, as Road Captain, designed all the best itineraries , safe and direct routes to use for any outlaw business. He spent five years in the local traffic police. But his lack of discipline and anger management issues made him fired. That's when he turned to Niall and wanted to be in. With all his knowledge on patrolling schedule, key points for road controls and safe locations. He is playing a pivotal role in the organisation, and usually good to meet customer and make a strong impression of good controls in place. He liked Aaron at the minute he saw him and he looks after him now, spending some time looking at maps and teaching him everything he knows. Niall has been watching them since the scene in the Nomads clubhouse when Aiden grabbed Aaron in his arms and told him he was proud of him. Connection like this could be very helpful for him, and that's why he sent Diarmuid to the Nomads. So it would put Aiden under pressure, and make him give more responsibilities to Aaron as some sort of trial.

Niall likes challenging people, give them more tasks, different objectives and see who he can rely on. That's how his officers went through the ranks. Showing dedication and commitment. The strength of the Rising Skulls is coming from the capacity to have the best man for each job, and the strongest team spirit possible. And that's how they have been always respected by the people. Because they had strong and professional members which always knew how to handle business in a proper way. And that's exactly the way Niall want's to handle things with Aaron. Have him taking over responsibilities by small bits, not having the official role of an officer so not having high expectations on him.

Despite that fact, leading the hang-around crew in the garage was already more than a prospect ever dealt with. And that's the topic of the discussion between Tom and Ian in the clubhouse. And the Operations Manager says:

- The kid is solid, that's a fact but he still has plenty to prove...

- You say that but Niall is giving him the garage to manage and he deals with one of our biggest customer now. The kid is already well made himself part of this organisation.

- Yes and I don't like that. He is a prospect and I think with the lads transferred to the Nomads, everyone forgot about that.

- We need everybody to step up now and be as strong as possible, two members away, that's not easy to fill up for them.

- I'm just saying we shouldn't forget he is not a member yet. He didn't go through half of the shit we went through you and me.

- Yeah but we were cleaning the clubhouse and collecting few hundred euros a month. He makes dozens of thousands a month, look after all our car and makes money through the garage too with outsiders.

- I'm maybe repeating myself, but let's be careful …

There is something in Tom's eyes that Ian spots as he looks at him. 'If that's not jealousy, then I don't know how is it called…' thinks Ian.

They still both look at Aaron, working and coordinating the garage. There is so much activity and everyone seems to be so well working together. Time to go on a run for the prospect, which gets into his SUV and leaves the club-house.

The routine goes on and on, Aaron dropping the car, smoking with the gate keeper, while he's loaded, and then getting his car dropped back and ready to go. He spent some time for the past three nights doing calculations on itineraries, based on his own experience and Aiden's advices and sharing. So here he is, looking at business like Usain Bolt looks at a 100 metres run. He likes competition, and he knows that better he will do his job, more satisfaction the customer will get and better will be his reputation in the Skulls organisation.

As he finishes his third cigarette and his second coffee, he sees the warehouse guys driving his car slowly towards the gate.

'Let's fucking do this', screams Aaron as he almost kicks the driver out of his car. Safety belt on, the gate is being opened. Time for the race. Tyres scream, engine roars, and his eyes focus. Arctic Monkeys in the CD player, the prospect starts to go through the industrial estate that he starts to know like his home town. All goes quickly around him, the road flies under his car. Almost reaching the first town, he gets closer and close from what seems to be a very old car. Trying to overlap it as fast as he can, the wheels go slightly into the side of the road and the car starts to slide. Controlling the SUV more or less, he finally gets back to the road. What should be scaring him just motivates him even more than he was before.

Not to catch attention of anyone, he drives low profile through town and as soon as the indicating shows that he left the town perimeter, he goes back to full speed. He overtakes more cars in this run than a grand-mother in a year. He feels the adrenaline rushing his heart beats.

One more kilometre to go, he's not looking at anything now aside of the road. There could be the Third World War around him; he wouldn't even notice it, as his eyes don't leave the road. Finally, he can see the consignee ware-house at the end of the road. Rocking into the industrial estate like he invades a country, Aaron pushes the engine one last time and breaks in front of the gate. Looking at his phone, he can see '38:07' and start screaming in his car: 'Thirty-eight minutes, fucking thirty-eight, I made it!'

Getting off his car and throwing the keys at the gate keeper now. Smile on his face, Aaron pulls his phone out of his pocket and calls Aiden:

- I fucking made it, 38 minutes and 7 seconds. You hear me?

- Great, son, well done… Are you done and available now?

- No, why? What's happening, you seem concerned?

67

- Ok, you don't move from there, I send you few Nomads to escort you. Are you carrying?

- No, of course not.

- Ok, I will tell the Nomads to drop you one. Wait for them; don't leave the site without them. They will escort you back to the clubhouse. Got it?

- Aye, got it. What the fuck is going on?

- We're officially in war soon. I'll fill you in when you're back home.

The euphoria dropped, and now Aaron walks inside the site thinking about Aiden's words … 'we're in war'. Who against? Why? What will happen now?

The time which was so fast in the car on his way to the warehouse is now slower than ever. And the Nomads are still not there. The security guard opens the warehouse gate while another guy is slowly driving Aaron's SUV out.

- Here you go, boy, grab your keys and get out, good job, says the guard.

- I will just hang around for a minute, I am waiting for my colleagues, won't be long.

- Well, sorry, boy, but your job is done, we can't let you stay on-site, and you know that.

-   Alright, will stay parked right in front of the entrance, okay?

-   Okay but no longer than 10 minutes.

The prospect gets in the car and calls Aiden as he drives away from the site. No answer to his call. He tries Tom. No answer either. 'What's happening to the clubhouse?'. He doesn't have the time to think any longer, that a dark car slows down in front of him. Impossible to look inside. The car stops for a second, engine still running, then leaves the place.

Chapter 5: The Rise of the Little Prince

The confusion doesn't have time to settle in his mind that Aaron sees two other cars arrive. Diarmuid in the first one with another guy next to him. Second car is having just one big driver in it. Diarmuid lowers his window and screams:

- What the fuck are you doing out of your car? Get in there and we will escort you back to the club-house.

- What about the gun?

- Which gun, kid?

- I don't carry shit, do you have one for me?

- Mother of Christ, what did they teach you at school? Here you go, take that and try not to shoot you.

After grabbing the gun that Diarmuid threw at him, Aaron runs into his car and drives. Diarmuid is up front with the Nomad heavily armed, Aaron drives second, and finally the last car is the Nomad on his own. The convoy runs through industrial estates, towns, countryside roads, like nothing could stop them. Finally arriving at the clubhouse, they park the cars inside and rush into the offices. All the Cork crew is there and most of the Nomads. The hang-around guys are grouped around the bar. Niall gets out of his office and says:

- All the officers and members, in my office! Nomads are welcome. Come on, brothers.

- Prospect, stay there, throws Tom smiling

As Aaron stays there watching all other members going into Niall's office, he sees Aiden looking above his shoulders and waving at him. People start looking at him and feel sorry to see him like that. Once the offices' doors are closed, he walks behind the bar and starts cleaning and sorting things. After ten minutes, noise raises from inside the offices with chairs moving and people walking. Doors open, all Nomads leave to the garage. Aaron looks at the open doors, no Cork guy leaving and no more noise.

- Aarooooon, come here, nooooow.

The voice of Diarmuid just froze the atmosphere in the room, which wasn't at its warmest already.

Aaron walks in, and looks at all his brothers sitting at the table.

No one smiling, staring at him.

- What … What can I do?

- Shut up and listen, says Tom looking at him darker than ever.

71

- Here is the situation, follows Niall. The Rising Skulls have always been looking after Cork, no other organisation ever really came around here and tried to settle. Now with all the business you have been part of, and all the money that it brought to the Skulls, it looks like the Devil Colony from Northern Ireland is looking to settle here. From what we saw there are at least 6 of their cars in town. We got intel that they are staying in three different locations in town and we need to raid all of them to clean the shit and send a strong message.

- What do you need from me?

- We have no time to waste with anyone, you know. The prospect status is making complications to our organisation, and we can't afford it anymore in these complicated times. You understand?

- What does it mean exactly?

- We had a vote, and wanted to get the Nomads to agree with it. You become a regular member as of today. You will work with me, Diarmuid, Sean, Ian and Lee. Aiden, Tom, Liam and Ceilin will be with the Nomads. Sean will give you the member patch, make sure to have it sewed and we will leave around 5pm. Any question?

- No, I'm good…

- Guys, let's get ready!

As everyone leaves the room, they all give a tap on the back or the head of Aaron, as a sort of welcome sign.

Everything went so quick and it was so unexpected for him. Everything seemed to live it so natural and he still doesn't realise what just happened. Sean walks towards him, grab his right hand, places the 'Rising Skulls' patch in it and closes the fingers.

- It's just the beginning, you better be ready, brother.

- I will. Thanks, brother.

Tom is still sitting at the table, and Aaron gets a sewing kit in the cabinet of the meeting room. Throwing his hoodies on the table to get the prospect patch off, the Vice-Manager stands up, walks slowly and confidently towards Aaron before moaning 'I'll be watching you, you won't have an easy life, boy' and leaving the room.

Aaron stays there, looking at him leaving, and knows he needs to focus and get ready. Once his patch is sewed, he goes to the garage and look at the cars... everything is ready, he instructs the hang-around crew to get them refilled in fuel and ready to go. Running to his room, he sees everyone else leaving their rooms, ready and armed like a little army ready to invade a country. He changes his shirt, puts his hoodies on, grab his gun and his chained wallet.

Walking out to the garage, the whole group is there waiting for him. Niall looks at him for few seconds, and then tells to the group:

- No mercy, no prisoners, we shoot to kill. Let me be extremely clear here. We take them out. Aaron, you drive the first car with me and Sean. Diarmuid, Ian and Lee in the second car. We will raid to the first location. At the same time, the Nomads will be with our third car composed of Aiden, Tom, Ceilin and Liam. You guys will take care about the second location. We get in there, do the job and drive as fast as possible. I don't know what their capacity for blowback is …

- And what happens if... starts Diarmuid

- It's not the time for questions, Diarmuid; it's the time for action and to protect our organisation. Let's go!

Everyone throw the bags in the trunks, and Aaron gets in his car. He goes first, and then Diarmuid follows him with the second car. They start to convoy with Aiden driving the third car and the Nomads in the last one. After few minutes in the town, Aaron and Diarmuid take the direction of the first house while the two other cars split towards the second one. In the car, no one talks; Aaron sets the music on an Arctic Monkeys album. He tries to look as relaxed and focused as possible. He's now a member, external weakness signs aren't the most popular around here and he needs to live with that. Niall's phone rings, that's Tom calling:

- Yeah, tell me.

- We arrived at the second house, are you still on your way?

- We should be there in few minutes. Keep your phone with you, I will let you now.

'Hurry up, Aaron, they arrived', says Niall after hanging up.

Flying through the last streets, the two cars arrive at destination. Niall sends a quick message to Tom then walks out of the car. They are in front of an old building, looking abandoned. All windows are closed and some planks are nailed to the window to block the access. Few cars are parked on the street, few meters away.

- That's the correct location, says Niall. Guys, get ready.

- Sun's out, guns out, responds Aaron, half smiling and grabbing his gun.

The second car parking in front of them, everyone regroups and start looking at the building, trying to find the best way to enter the block. Diarmuid steps in:

- Ok, first team in the front, second team in the back. Anything you see, you don't think twice and you shoot. These guys are up for a war, no doubt about that.

- Remember, lads, no prisoner, no mercy, no survival.

After a long silence, Aaron stops the group:

- What if we don't have to attack and just have to eradicate them like bugs?

- What are you talking about? Says Niall, looking totally confused.

- The gas tank next to the house. We make it blow, they will panic and just think about running out of the block. Half of them may not even have weapons on them as they go out...

Everyone looks at him like it is an alien.

- Come on, guys, we ain't a commando group. Let's get the rats leave the sinking boat.

- You better be right, Aaron. Second team, in the back, Diarmuid, you on the side to shoot at that tank and the first team stays in front. Split to cover as much surface as we can.

The voice of Niall is stronger than ever. Aaron knows that if the plan succeeds and there is no damage or injury for any member, it will be a big victory for him. Niall calls Tom, in charge of the operations for the second location. 'Tom, it's on'. Not waiting on any response, he hangs up the phone and shows a thumb up to the second team to go around the building. Everyone in position, looking at Diarmuid. He shoots. Nothing. Absolutely nothing happens. He shoots again, a metallic sound indicates the impact of the bullet.

- If they hear the impacts they will know we are here says Aaron to Niall.

- I know, any idea, Einstein?

- Leave it with me, boss.

Aaron opens the trunk of the car and grabs a small fuel container. He runs towards the building front and throws fuel around the gas tank, and runs next to Diarmuid.

- Time to set the place on fire, brother.

- What the hell are you doing, Aaron?

Taking his shirt out, Aaron puts it around the fuel container and grabs his lighter. The whole team looks at him with the feeling that something wrong is going to happen.

Aaron lights his 'package' on fire and throws it at the gas tank. An immense flame is now burning all over the tank.

- Wait a minute and shoot again, the shit is gonna blow up.

Running back to the team, he can only notice that all eyes are on him, as no one really understands what he is doing. The smoke starts to be darker and darker. Diarmuid gets ready. Aaron's heart is beating like a drum in a rock concert. Then the shot. Straight into the tank. And then the sound of the explosion. Everyone closed their eyes and felt the vibration. As he stands above the car, Niall looks at the scene. Fire on the side of the block, smoke all over the place, which looks more like a Vietnam's war scene than a daily Cork City view.

- Everyone splits, come on, lads, let's do this!

He looks behind him, Aaron is standing and splitting the crew. No time to think, the main door of the building opens quickly and two guys run through it. The Rising Skulls don't wait and open the fire on them, and quickly the two body drop dead on the ground. The fire intensifies on the side of the building, but no one else seems to be leaving it.

Diarmuid walks slowly around the block to reach Niall's position:

- What should we do, boss, no one gets out of there anymore.

- I don't know, what about you ask G.I Aaron here, responds Niall smiling and turning around.

- Well, as you kindly ask me, I would say, firefighters are surely on their way, Police too, so either we attack right now or we fuck off.

The silence sets in the group, everyone looking at each other waiting for someone to make a move. Aaron stands, looks around and people are starting to approach the scene closer and closer.

- Call the second team, let's go!

As the first team gets into the car, police cars' hooters are approaching and still no sign of the second team. Niall is trying to get them on the phone, no answer.

- What are they doing, these idiots?

- Should I go and check, proposes Diarmuid

- If you like the idea of spending the next 10 years in jail, go for it, answers Aaron. Let's give them a minute.

The first police cars are arriving on the other end of the streets. A head pops up from the building corner, then a second one, both looking around checking if the crossing of the street is safe.

Everyone in Aaron's car is screaming to hurry up. The second team throw themselves in the car. Aaron, engines on, is ready to go. Bu the police cars approach so close that he knows he needs to do something to delay block them from stopping the whole group. Niall is next to him screaming, Sean is grabbing his gun. Hand-brake off, first gear on, he rushes the SUV towards the police cars. Everything goes so fast around him. 'No time to hesitate', he thinks to himself. He grabs and pulls up the hand-brake, turns the wheel, and the car does a 90 degrees shift, the sound of tyres mixing with Sean screaming in the back.

The three police cars stop, engines still on, while cops are pointing their guns towards Niall and Sean, which are the first ones in their sight. Aaron looks back at Diarmuid, he is ready to go.

- What is the plan now? Asks Sean.

- Ladies and gents, time to fuck off, screams Aaron. Hold on!

As he drives the car out of there, the second team shoots in direction of the police to stop them for few seconds. Diarmuid starts right behind Aaron in a storm of dust and noise.

- Maybe it's time to check how the other group is doing, hope it's better than us, proposes Sean.

- It can't be worse than us anyway, responds Niall. Will give them a call.

No one answers on the phone on the third car. Nomads phone are all switched off too.

- Aaron, you better be driving home ASAP, can't reach anyone. I'll tell Diarmuid to take care of the cops.

Engine and tyres screaming while the second car open fires on the cops, Aaron gets quickly to the clubhouse. Nomads and the third car are there, everyone chilling and smoking. Niall gets his gun out, runs out of the car in direction to the President of the Nomads:

- What the hell were you doing not answering your phone? We were struggling like idiots out there and you weren't able to pick up your god damn mobiles?

- There is no cell coverage here since we got back. We got there 10 minutes ago, the address you sent us too was a dead end, no one was there and we just came back here waiting for you.

- For Christ sake, everything went south for us over there, we didn't manage to smoke them out of the house and the police came up, Diarmuid is still there getting rid of them I suppose… Aaron, get in here!

The whole group splits and Aaron walks his way towards Niall:

- Yeah? Says Aaron

- Can you tell me what the hell happened over there?

- I tried to be creative!

- Creative? You're not Pablo fucking Picasso, you idiot, we do business here, we were going to assault a building, not to do anything fancy!

- Oh yes? And what was the plan, heh? We got in there with fuck all plan, nothing, not a clue of what we were supposed to do. And yet that's my fault?

- Enough! I don't care about what you're saying, YOU took the responsibility to lead the team, YOU made a mistake, and YOU are responsible for that mess.

Aaron's face is completely frozen, his eyes are burning, and his breathe his loud and deep. Niall shakes his head to tell him to leave the room.

As Aaron makes his way out towards the clubhouse, the rest of the members are regrouping around Niall. The garage door opens, and Diarmuid's car rushes inside in a storm of tyres and engine noises.

- Are you all okay? What happened over there? Asks the Director.

- I had to shoot two cops in the legs and burn an oil barrel on the road, that was fucking Bagdad out there when we left, answers Ian.

- I wasn't talking to you! Screams Niall

- What's wrong with you, yells Diarmuid back to him.

- We need to figure out how to turn that situation around. I'm quite sure the patrols recognised and it's a matter how hours before they do something here.

While everybody start thinking about an idea, the clubhouse door opens up and Aaron runs down the stairs towards the group.

- Everybody in the car, I know how to sort that out, come on let's go!

- Aaron, for Christ sake, what are you doing?

Niall doesn't have the time to say more that the group jumps back in the cars. He still stands in front of Aaron's car. Arron screams:

- You wanted me to do business, then get in that car and let's do business.

- You're just the gift that keeps on giving…

Tyres screaming, the cars leave the warehouse and run down the streets of the town.

- So are you going to explain me what's going on and why do I have my entire crew rushing out now?

- When we were there, shooting to that house, I noticed two grey vans parked on the street, for the same Plumber company. I checked on internet now and they aren't located anywhere nearby that neighborhood, but that company is registered just nearby the second house. That must be their base for all the business. We go there, we blow the whole damn place and we take back what is ours.

- Ok that's great work but how do we know if we will have enough!

- It's business, Niall, it's not exact science. I won't stay home waiting for shit to fall on us.

Street after street, the tension rises inside the cars, nobody talks and Aaron keeps on speeding. The other cars behind him, he finally slows down when turning into the destination street. The two grey vans are parked in front of what seems to be a very old Plumber shop.

- Ok so the vans are here, there is nobody outside watching. There doesn't seem to have any backyard or exit anywhere. What do you suggest, Niall?

- Oh now you ask for instructions after? Anyway... Nomads to prepare the scene with long-range rifles and we get in there to clean the rest. Get them on the phone.

Lee gives his phone to Niall and everybody aligns on the strategy. Nomads walk out of their cars and walk slowly and carefully opposite the shop, hidden behind cars. Once in position, they wave to Aiden that runs as closely to the walls as possible followed by the rest of the crew. Everybody stops few yards back from the door. Aaron is about to wave at the Nomads to get them opening fire when suddenly, the door opens and a man casually walks out, lightening up a cigarette. Ceilin runs from the back of the group, grabs his knife and stab him straight into his back. And again. And again. The man slowly falls from Ceilin's arms on the ground. There is a big silence on the street.

A gun is fired. Ceilin drops dead in a fragment of a second. Then the street goes back into its silence. Sean wants to run to Ceilin but Niall stops him. Everybody freezes. Aaron tries to ask the Nomads if they see anything. Negative answer. He turns then to Niall and says "that's my fault if all goes to shit, I'm going first". As he stands and starts walking towards the door, he knocks on the shoulder of Aiden to tell him to follow. He sends the signal to the Nomads, which rise above cars and start firing through the shop windows. After 10 intense seconds, they all stop to get ammunition. Second wave incoming. This is like hell on Earth. There is wood and glass all over the walk-path. The second firing is under way as Aaron grabs a piece of glass to try and see what's inside the shop. The reflection isn't great and doesn't help him much.

- Aiden, I'll run towards the opposite wall to catch their attention, you stay in this corner, get your head out and fire anything that moves. Ok?

- Alright, got your back, brother.

As Aaron throws himself in the shop, Aiden pops his head inside and doesn't see anything. No one in there, dead or alive. Both don't move and stay still. The rest of the group gets in. Aiden and Aaron progress together at the back in what looks like a storage room. Still not a sign of anyone or anything moving. The confusion reigns across the team and everybody look back and start walking towards to street.

- Hold it, whispers Aaron, grabbing Aiden's arm.

- What's going on, Aaron?

- Look on the ground. Blood. Someone is still here.

They both follow a blood track, while everybody walks away. This seems to lead them back to the storage room, into some sort of massive metal cabinet.

- No time to take a risk, says Aaron, as he raises his gun.

- Don't kill him for Christ sake

- That asshole killed Ceilin.

Pointing the gun in direction of the cabin. One shot. And a second one. Within seconds Sean arrives running and screaming. He finds Aaron still pointing his gun at the cabinet while Aiden goes to open the doors.

The doors open and some blood drips through. Then a body completely drops on the ground in front of the entire crew that now got back into the room.

The man, with a long beard and military outfit, is hardly breathing and not moving at all, like paralysed.

Niall moves towards him:

- Aiden, finish him.

- But boss, he is dead already, what's the point?

- He is breathing, and I'm telling you to finish him.

- Wait a minute and he is d..

Aiden doesn't have the time to finish his sentence that Aaron terminates the guy firing a bullet in his head. The prospect looks at Niall and says "that's alright, now he is dead" before walking away.

The Director keeps on looking at Aiden. That's the first time that Aiden says no to an order. Everybody finds the Nomads and Aaron out on the street smoking.

"There is no police coming to us and the Nomads didn't intercept any radio message mentioning the shooting so we better get our ass out of here before it all goes South for us."

Everybody gets back to the clubhouse and Niall calls for a meeting immediately.

"Aaron, you're going to sit that one out, I'll fill you in later".

He doesn't give him a chance to answer and walks in the boardroom. Tom closes the doors behind him and the silence settles in the clubhouse. Aaron sits down on one of the couch and while he hears the noise level rising in the room, he can't understand what's being said. Minutes are passing, doors are still closed. "This sounds like I'm in the Vatican waiting for the white smoke to announce the nomination of the new

pope.", thinks Aaron. 25 minutes passed. 26... 27... 28... Still nothing. Still sitting. And still waiting. The most irritating is that he is waiting without knowing what he is waiting for. Might be nothing to do with him. While he is making his third coffee, he hears the gavel. Nobody seems to move though. A chair moves. Someone is now walking. Niall opens the doors and finds Aaron starring at him with his coffee mug in one hand and a pack of cookies in the other hand.

- Once you'll be finished with your breakfast, get in here. We've got to talk.

- No but I was just…

Once again the director doesn't let him finish what he's saying and turn around. Aaron walks towards him while the room is in a complete silence. The young man looks at his boss while he can feel the entire crew looking at him.

- So, says Aaron, are you gonna tell me what's that all about?

- If you would be as smart as you're impatient, boy, you would be just the full package, aye? Answers Liam.

- Enough, continues Niall. So, Aaron, we discussed the matter and there is clearly a need for a change in this organisation in regards of the security management. Our security officer is battling on all fronts and with the support he gave to the Nomads lately, it's not fair to expect even further. So we voted and agreed that going forward, you will be the new Security Lead for the Cork branch. Business is growing and outsider threat grows with it, so days like today are needing what you did today. Creativity, courage and efforts. You stood up for what you thought would be good for us and I respect that. Obviously you have to learn to listen more and communicate better but I guess that will come with time.

- Sounds good to me! responds Aaron while the rest of the crew are hitting the table to cheer him up.

Niall taps the new Security Lead on the back and hands over to him the 'Enforcer' patch.

- Get that on your hoodie and we can keep it going.

Chapter 6: Vesuvius

There hasn't been a day since Aaron joined the Skulls without thinking 'Is this worth the risk? Am I going anywhere in here?'. Well, the Enforcer patch on his hoodie answers all of the questions. When waking up morning after morning, he can now see the difference of behaviour around him, people change the way they talk to him, and he is now having a vote at the table. Even Tom, which has always been refractory to having him around, is now a bit more relaxed.

The club got into a fairly stable routine, few news prospects joined after Tom started to recruit. The garage is running at its full capacity and that bring a consequent amount of cash to the organisation, while making it look like a clean-ish company from the outside. Locals know what's happening behind closed doors, but they all benefit from having a local organisation that looks after them and keep the city as safe as it can be.

Niall, Diarmuid and Aaron have been discussing few times already on some improvement initiatives to gain prosperity and stability on the Security business. There hasn't been much additional business coming in lately and with the new prospects joining the team, the need for a bigger cash flow is growing.

Diarmuid proposed to create truck assaults on the motorway to increase the need for escort services across the industries. There are hi-tech, pharmaceuticals, retails products every day and night and that's not the local police that will be looking out for people anyway.

Niall is quite supportive of the idea; make it happen through the Nomads group, as they aren't attached anywhere so their faces isn't as familiar for people as the sedentary members' are. In the next two days, the final decision will be up for a vote. There has not been any tough discussion to settle for in a while. Aaron and Diarmuid are chatting up around a coffee in the clubhouse:

- I don't like it, and I don't want it, says the Enforcer. That's a mistake… We are cruising, there is no one causing us any trouble, business is not big enough but we aren't out on the street either. I'm just saying, this could be dangerous to provoke something outside of our control.

- Listen, whatever is decided tomorrow, we will make it work. We always did, and will always do.

The clubhouse became more and more political with the importance of each vote to get this decision passing. Everybody tries to know what each member is going to vote and influence people which aren't having the same opinion. Tom decided to clearly go against Diarmuid and Niall, which doesn't help the organisation to stick as a whole. Aiden has not been consulted much while being the Road

Officer. That doesn't go unnoticed. And he is standing in the room behind Aaron and Diarmuid:

- Nobody asked me anything. I used to be considered and valued for what I know and what I have to say. Nobody gives a shit anymore around here. Whatever happens in this vote doesn't matter too much to be honest. This club needs a change, and sooner rather than later.

- Easy tiger, answers Diarmuid. Why don't you stop being overly reactive and stick with your club? The vote will give us a decision, we will handle it, and everything will be just fine.

- Is that what you really want? For real? Continues Aiden. Because I can tell you right now. We don't have the bandwidth to handle that. Plain and simple.

After a long silence, Diarmuid walks closer to Aiden and says:

- If you have a problem, just go out and say it, but stop moaning like a little girl while nobody is watching.

The rest of the conversation sounds like a copy-paste of the same arguments again and again. And again. Meanwhile, Aaron grabs few members to go and help at the garage and avoid more club members getting into the discussion. Tom has refused to pick a side and since he made that statement, he avoids small talks as much as possible. Barely present in the garage, always have to go out for 'meetings'. The Nomads are checking in almost everyday and there is now no doubt they are trying to convince and buy some votes inside the clubhouse.

Sean, Lee and Ian have been on a lot of jobs lately. Small businesses have faced an increasing amount of security issues, but it is not where the big money is. These three members have seen lots of stability for many years while all the recent changes seem to affect them. They have a vote at the table but they hardly make any decision that will really influence the club's future.

Ian tried few times to bring new business at the table but his lack of vision has always made him being seen as naive by his brothers. Lee has always been the quiet one which would be laid back and waits for people to tell him what to do. When Sean joined the club as a prospect, he was about 15 years old, could hardly go through a day without drinking and was smoking two packs a day. Niall took the kid with him everyday to show him there was better things to do than drinking and smoking. Like becoming an outlaw, a gang member. But becoming as well a part of something, a crew, a family, have responsibilities towards each other. He had a bit of a meltdown when his girlfriend broke up with him last year and decided to leave with their dog to the other side of the world. Once again, Niall was there to pick him up and involve him in jobs that would maintain his head above water. People can never really tell if Niall is genuine or if these are calculated moves to buy votes whenever he needs them. On reflection, Sean has never voted against his Director. And that's just one example.

Vote is imminent and all these stories are more than ever present in members' minds. Aaron is walking out of his shower when he hears Niall and Tom having a one-to-one conversation in the lockers room.

- So where are we with the votes?

- Diarmuid, you and Sean are a Yae. Aiden and Aaron and a Nae. I have proxy for Liam, he is a Nae. Ian and Lee are undecided from what I could hear.

- Okay. It's almost 1 o'clock. Meeting is at 3. Which means we have two hours to convince them both. I need that vote to go the right way. I have to pay a visit to a customer.

- I won't get that job done for you. I'm not sure yet where I'm at on this one.

- Fine, if I have to, I'll sort that out myself. I am not sure I can count on you for anything anymore.

Aaron is still there, standing in his towel, listening to the conversation. After a few seconds of complete silence, Niall walks out. And within seconds, Tom throws a chair against the wall, which breaks in a massive noise. Now it's the Operations Manager's turn to leave the room.

The Security Lead knows it, it's time for him to make Ian and Lee's minds towards a negative vote. After getting dressed, he heads to the garage. Empty. No car, no member, only finding Luke standing next to Lisa. The boy holds one of his toy and while he gets closer, his dad can hear him crying:

- Hey, little man, what's wrong? Why are you crying like that?

- He's had a really bad day at school, and I think you should talk to him, answers Lisa.

- Ok. Luke, can you tell to Daddy what happened today? Follows Aaron.

- The... The... The other kids. They are mean. They are saying my daddy kills people and is a bad daddy.

Luke keeps crying while his parents are looking at each other. Aaron grabs his little boy in his arms:

- Okay listen to me. Daddy is a good man. Daddy fixes broken cars, and helps people, and protects people around him. Your daddy doesn't do bad thing, you know.

The look of Lisa to her man says it all. She knows he is lying, but she wants their son to feel better.

- Luke, why don't you go and play upstairs on the couch, Mommy and Daddy just need to talk, says Aaron while dropping his son back down.

Once he walked upstairs, Aaron feels a massive hit behind his head:

- See what you're doing! Your kid is 4 and he already gets shit at school because of you. And what do you think happens to me, huh? People call me all sort of things because of you. It's on you, ON YOU!

- Okay are you done? Now give me a minute.

Aaron walks upstairs and closes the door behind him leaving her all alone in the garage. Few minutes pass. The door finally reopens. Luke runs through the stairs with a white package in his hands.

- What's this, sweetheart, is it for me?

- Daddy said it will make you happy.

- Ok, says Lisa opening the letter. Let's see if your Daddy knows me well.

The envelop is full of cash. All in €20 and €50 bills.

- Baby, can you go back upstairs. Daddy and Mommy need to have another discussion.

- Yes, mommy.

Once again, they wait for the boy to be upstairs:

- So that's what you think I'm here to see? That's what I am looking for?

- This covers you and our son for the end of this month and for the following month already!

- I don't need your dirty money! I want my man and my boy, all together, all happy. I'm not asking you anything else than that.

- Are we gonna have that conversation again? You weren't happy. You were having two jobs and thinking of a third one. I was working so much I hardly saw our son growing..

- You don't even see us at all now, I should get your mail forwarded here!

- All I can think is that you got that money by killing people or stealing it somehow. I'm telling you, come back home. Please.

The garage doors open and several cars rush inside.

- Oh great, continues Lisa. Looks like your new family is here. I'll grab OUR son and go back to OUR home. Keep your money. And if you want to keep me and your son in your life somehow, you better do something.

Before Aaron has time to answer anything, they are surrounded by members jumping off the cars. And a blonde girl is with them. Someone Aaron never saw before but has something familiar. Looking at Aaron and Lisa, Diarmuid asks:

- We're okay here?

- We are perfect, answers Lisa.

Everyone walks silently to the clubhouse or unloading cars. Lisa grabs Luke in her arms and starts walking away while she hears the blonde girl says:

- Hey, you must be Aaron, so nice to finally meet you!

Aaron's girlfriend turns her head around and if a look could kill, they would be already preparing Aaron's funerals. He looks back at her surprised, trying to show her he doesn't know that girl.

The Security Lead looks at the car, they are in really bad shape. Bullet holes, windows broken dirt and mud everywhere. The garage team is going to be busy. He gives few calls to get the crew over and start fixing the vehicles but he knows he will have to work on it as well.

He opens up the trunk of Diarmuid's truck, and he can see two bodies wearing club's hoodies. One is a prospect from the Nomad crew, impossible to see the face of the second corpse. That explains why everyone was so silent and he decides to walk upstairs to find out what happens. Lee tells him straight:

- It was an ambush, a massacre. Blood everywhere, we lost two at least, Nomads are really pissed off.

- Who did it? Do we know?

- No idea, kid, but we will get to the bottom of it.

The rest of the night is about working on cars, smoking cigarettes and baring with this awkward silence across the clubhouse. It's finally 4:30 in the morning when the garage quiets down. Aaron sends the mechanics up to the clubhouse for a coffee and a shower.

He lights another cigarette, turns on the radio and sits down on the stairs. The garage is really dark, with most of the lights switched off now. The clubhouse door opens behind him.

- Here he is! I was looking for you. We haven't been introduced yet. Erin, Erin Bradley.

- Niall's daughter, is it?

- You bet I am. That makes me your boss, basically.

- Unless you're called Niall, Tom or Diarmuid, you are not my boss. End of story.

- Hmmm dodgy, just how I like my boy.

- I think you saw my girlfriend and my kid, no?

- I saw your boy, yeah. Now I'm not sure if you should call her your girlfriend anymore based on how she was looking at you.

- What are you doing up so late? follows Aaron.

- I'm not much of a sleeper.

- Aye, I get that…

They spend most of the rest of the night sitting on the stairs, chatting away and drinking rum.

Around 7am, Lee, Aiden and Niall walk out of the club-house to find Erin asleep on the stairs, while Aaron fits new tyres on his car.

The Director stares at Aaron, while Lee and Aiden laughs at his face.

- You don't want to know what happened in this garage, boss, let's go! says Aiden with a cheeky smile.

- Aaron, grab your stuff, we're leaving, instructs Niall.

- Give me a minute, boss, I'll be right there.

The Security Lead has just the time to change his t-shirt, grab a take-away coffee in the kitchen and run down the stairs. The boss starts briefing everyone on the situation. The Club has never faced such a confrontation and they are about to go to War against something they have no clue of its dimension. They might be a dozen, they might be a hundred. The garage door opens, and a pick-up truck rushes inside. The men stepping out of it are all dressed like military troops. The driver of the truck walks towards Niall:

- I assume you're the man in charge?

- And who I should be assuming I'm talking to?

- We are just a few guys that heard you were in trouble. I'm pretty sure we can come in handy to help retaliate.

- And why would you help us? We don't know you, you don't know us, what's in there for you?

- Well, we aren't gonna do that for free, are we? I like to see ourselves are entrepreneurs seising opportunities.

- Don't flatter yourself, you're just a soldier that takes credit cards.

The two men are staring at each other. They know they need each other, but none wants to look weaker. They both go back to the clubhouse to discuss the details. Meanwhile, in the garage, the Skulls and the soldiers are standing in silence.

The clock is ticking, without anyone knowing if it's a good or bad thing, if their enemies are ready to strike again or if they are gone.

After a few more discussions, Niall shakes hands with their leader and the brief kicks off. Everything is discussed: location, positions, striking order, weapons used, cars itineraries. Whatever they do, they have to do it now. Being on the front foot in this situation is key, and everyone knows it. Few members start making calls to their local contacts to find out any information that could be useful. Names, affiliations, partnerships, relationships, type of business. Anything is good to know or could be used in the preparations. Aaron organises together with Diarmuid lining up all weapons available on the main table of the meeting room, with ammunition and all equipment. No place for mistakes today. The clubhouse is completely buzzing, with friends and hang-arounds coming to help as well. Aaron turning his back to the meeting room entrance, he doesn't notice anything special when someone enters the room. A hand touches his left shoulder and he hears someone saying:

- I should tell my Dad he makes you work too hard, Aaron. You look like you need a break.

- What.. what are you doing here, Erin?

- Well, nothing special, just came and say hi. I would happily help you out if you need a hand with anything.

- I appreciate the offer but I have a lot of work still to do, I have to go.

- Alright, alright, sorry to bother, Mister Serious. I'm leaving.

Aaron turns back to the table counting the rounds of ammunition, when he feels being grabbed by the shoulder. Instinctively he turns his head around and feels a mouth smoothly kissing his left cheek.

'Take care of yourself, Busy Boy'. It was Erin, before leaving the room for good and leaving him alone.

A minute later, another hand grabs his shoulder

- Alright Erin this time where are you going to kiss, for Christ's sake.

Niall is standing there, with Tom and the mercenaries' leader.

- We will talk about that later, Aaron. In the meantime, let me introduce you to Sandro, him and his team will help us. How are things looking around here?

-   We are going to be short on ammunition, especially around AK-47 rounds. We will be fine with guns' ones. Hand grenades, only a few left. I've reached out to our suppliers to see if there is any stock left but nothing came back yet. I've found a few other equipment in stock, like this bad boy!

He opens long black case, and takes a sniper riffle out of it. It's covered in dust, just as much as the case is.

-   I've enough ammunition for that one to invade Iraq by myself, so I'll give all my other gear to the rest of the team and dust this thing off.

-   Son, are you out of your mind? When was the last time you shot with that?

-   That's the beauty of it, I guess, last time someone fired it, I was probably still warm and cozy in my mother's belly.

-   Aaron, you've done a great job with preparing it all, but that's just stup-...

-   Niall, I'm not asking here, just telling you, that's what I will go out with today. Now... Are we ready to go or what?

Tom leads them back to the garage, everyone standing there, like preachers waiting for the priest on Sunday mornings. Aaron and Tom walk down the stairs to join the group.

Niall just addresses the crowd, reinforcing the message, the purpose, the sense of responsibility towards the community. And finishes his speech by 'I cannot guarantee you'll all be back to your families tonight, say goodbye before we leave'.

The atmosphere is quite tense as everyone boards the cars and prepare to leave. Drivers align one last time on the road map. Aaron, Diarmuid, and Aiden and a couple of Nomads are around the garage table with the city map. Aiden is in charge of the talk:

- We will hit North for about 25 minutes before it starts to worry me. Don't forget that we've never really got into that part of town. You won't get much familiar faces around you. The garage crew installed overnight some new toys on your car. State-of-the-art digital satellite navigation devices. Few locations have been saved in there. The one we are going to strike, and few other safe houses that I've hand picked for us. Under no circumstances we get back here unless we know it's 100% safe to do so. Thanks to Aaron and his team for prepping the car.

- New tyres, new brakes, new suspensions, fuel refilled, reinforced windshields, additional space cre-
  ated everywhere in the vehicles for better transpor-
  tation, continues Aaron. The team did an amazing
  job, let's make sure we do our job now, shall we.

Maps folded, guns ready, nervous faces on. The drivers
shake hands and board now their cars. A hang-around is
walking towards the garage door to make way for the cars
while Erin comes to Aaron's window.

- What do you want now, Erin?

- So I am not allowed to kiss you good luck, am I?

- Alright, quickly then.

Aaron shows her his right cheek and she executes herself
then walk back one step.

- Get back here so I can give you another one.

Aiden leads the convoy, with Aaron closing it. Seven vehicles is not discreet in any way. Within minutes they exit
the town and hit straight onto the motorway. No radio on
the car, and no one talking.

Last motorway junction, next up on the road is an industrial estate to go through. It's Sunday, all warehouses are
closed, and streets are empty. It's the perfect place for an
ambush.

'Guns out, boys, something doesn't feel right around here' screams Aiden on the walkie talkie.

It takes a good few minutes for the convoy to go through the estate. Suddenly a car comes out of nowhere and cut the convoy in half. All vehicles stop and everyone rushes out with guns ready to shoot. The whole scene looks like a police intervention.

- Step out of the car, now! Screams a Nomad.

- Show me your hands, show me your fucking hands, shouts another one.

The two people inside the car aren't moving. Hands are up. Impossible to see their faces properly, nor if they wear any organisation colors.

Aaron grabs the sniper rifle and aims at the car. Tom sees his move and waves his right arm to stop him from shooting.

The whole convoy is on standby. The two individuals inside the stranger's car are still no moving, still keeping their hands up.

Niall sends Diarmuid to check from closer range. The security officer waves at a couple of Nomads to close in the car slowly from the back. Ian starts telling his Director 'I don't like that, something feels wrong, the guys in the car, that's so weird'. Aaron re-aims at the car and zooms in on the driver of the car. 'The driver has a mouth gag. DIAR-MUID, THE DRIVER HAS A MOUTH GAG, STOOOOP', he shouts.

And as Diarmuid looks back in Aaron's direction, a big explosion emerges from the car to blow it completely on fire, with the deflagration hitting the cars and the buildings around. Niall looks over the car and sees bodies on the ground. 'Let's go!', he shouts at everyone to go and check who is on the ground.

Sean arrives the first near the bodies to realise that Diarmuid didn't make it, blood everywhere around his head. One of the nomad didn't make it either, the other one breathes but his eyes are closed and the blood stain on his shirt increases very quickly. The car is burning heavily. Tom orders the Nomads to put the bodies of the deceased members into the back of their car.

Aaron snaps at Niall:

-   Maybe next time I want to shoot at a car that just rushed into our convoy, you won't stop me so we can save our brothers' lives.

-   We will discuss about this later, continues Niall. It's weird they target us with a car like that but there is nobody else is coming at us now.

- Maybe they want us to carry on the mission, and this was just the appetiser of what they have prepared for us, adds Sean. We are three guys down and we didn't even make it yet to our destination.

- Going back to the garage now doesn't make too much sense either, does it, intervenes Lee. We started this, let's finish it. It won't get better by postponing it to tomorrow or the next day. Let's go!

- Whatever feels wrong, we shoot. No more

Everyone gets back into the cars, guns in hand and aimed at the outside of the respective windows. The convoy gets back moving and after 15 minutes, the destination is in sight. All cars get the message from Niall to stop. Everyone comes out and it's time for one last quick briefing. Everyone is clear on roles and responsibilities, cars get back on the move. What looks like a disaffected compound soon shows some signs of moves inside.

'Everyone, heads down and hang in there' scream Tom as he drives the first car through the main barriers. The windshield breaks and the engine roars as the car gets stuck in the barriers few meters inside the compound. Meanwhile, Aiden, Aaron, Joe and the mercenary car drive around Tom's car to make their way inside. Aiden drives very fast into the targeted building, right in the middle of the compounds. The big warehouse seems to have only a couple of doors, the rest of the building being made of loading bays for trucks.

110

Aaron takes the opposite side around the building, with Joe and the mercenaries staying on the main parking lot. Ian and Liam are on the phone to coordinate when the different teams will penetrate the building.

'3...2...1... GO' and they shoot with silenced handguns to destroy the door locks.

Aaron leads his team, while Niall and Joe make their own way into the building via the other doors. He can hear loud voices in the background like people arguing, but no noise signalising they would be preparing themselves. The Security Lead grabs his sniper rifle to look at the targets... Everyone is sitting down, talking with each other.

'Tell the others to throw grenades in the middle and to move in straight after' tells Aaron to Liam who had the phone.

After Liam confirms back that everyone got the instruction, the Nomads throw hand grenades and straight after the series of explosion, everyone raises from behind the pallets they were using as cover to see who is still there. There is an army, probably about 50 men, standing or falling in the middle, victims of the grenades. Based on the look of these men, they got caught by surprise.

Joe screams 'TAKE THEM DOOOOOWN' as everyone starts emptying their guns' magazines. Bodies are dropping heavily in the middle of the warehouse.

After a couple of minutes of intense firing, everyone stops and the silence settles again in the warehouse. Slowly, all the members are moving out of their bidding places and walk towards the pile of bodies and the lake of blood that forms itself on the ground.

Niall sees one body still moving, and when he walks towards it to hopefully get some answers on the origins of this gang, Sean shoots him straight into his head.

- Die, bitch

- I guess we won't be asking him questions, continues Tom, walking towards the same body.

- Let's grab all the weapons, there is a decent stock here, that would be very useful in the future, says Niall.

Tom and Aaron bring cars to the loading gates while Nomads start piling up guns, rifles and all military equipment they can find.

Meanwhile the mercenaries are looking in the offices for any paperwork or clue who are these people.

- What are we doing of all these bodies? There are a lot of them, says Sean.

- Well, I don't know. It seems we wiped out the whole crew. Can we use this location in the future?, answers Niall.

- Let's keep a team on site while we run a quick background check and see who owns the place and we can then decide what we do, continues Sean It's secluded enough, discreet, and we only have the doors and the main gate to change and we are good to go.

The mercenaries come back with a few invoices from suppliers but nothing giving any specifics on this organisation.

A couple of hours later, everyone gets back in the cars, bar Lee, Liam and a couple of Nomads. They will stay onsite and start cleaning up the mess, keep piling up bodies, and search the building even further to try and find more information.

The silence in the cars on the way back to the garage is complete. The death of Diarmuid is something that will heart the organisation. He has always been a trusted advisor to Niall and a good voice to balance Tom's occasional irrational views and opinions. He was there from the very beginning of the organisation and that's what is on everyone's mind.

Arriving at the garage, everyone walking out of the cars, with friends and family kept in the clubhouse, Erin walks out towards Niall first, and jumps in his arms. Then looks at Aaron, who's face still has blood stains from the blast of the grenades.

- Are you okay babe?, she asks.

- I'm okay. But we lost Diarmuid and a couple of Nomads. It's all over now, though. We should all be safe hopefully.

Erin turns back to Niall:

- I'm so sorry for Diarmuid, he was such a good man.

- We will organise a nice ceremony, continues Niall. He deserves everyone to pay their respect. I want it packed, friends, family, members from all charters and all affiliates. We will do it here, in a couple of days. Sean! Please coordinate the ceremony and the invites. I'm going to bed.

Still in complete silence, all the members are emptying the cars from all the weapons they have loaded at the warehouse, and then carry the three bodies of their fallen brothers into an abandoned white van in a corner of the garage.

'We always knew there were risks associated with what we are doing, I just thought it would not happen to the best of us' thought Aaron to himself as he washes out Diarmuid's blood from the back of his SUV.

Chapter 7: Love after all

It's Tuesday morning. Aaron opens his eyes, but he cannot realise where he is. Still very sleepy, with one eye closed, he rolls on his side to look at his surroundings. An old oak table, a bookshelf, a massive cabinet that is as high as the ceiling is. Then a television, another big cabinet and what looks like a giant basket that is most likely a dog bed. Getting up from what seems to have been his bed for the night - a couch- , he still cannot figure out where he is. In the corner of the room, there is a door, so he walks towards it after grabbing his mobile phone and his gun that were lying on the floor next to his sleeping location.

Walking out the room, finding himself in a dark corridor, the confusion remains high and he tries to remember from the night before what brought him there and where he actually is. Somehow he hears some noise behind a door, which he decides to open, his gun well ready to be fired if necessary. However, what he finds behind the door is definitely not calling for violence, and is anything but stranger to him.

Erin is preparing breakfast, all dressed in black and at the table of what is clearly the kitchen of Niall's house.

- Hey sleepy face, I made you bacon and eggs, and pancakes. Sit down, I'll serve you some.

- Babe, how come did I sleep here? I can't remember much about last night.

- You fell in the garage while working on the cars, Sean thought you were exhausted so we brought you here to keep an eye on you. Of course, Dad didn't want the two of us to sleep in the same bed...

- Alright, cool, thanks... Why are you dressed like that?

- It's Diarmuid's funerals today, you remember?

As Aaron finally starts to put together all the pieces of his day, he realises he needs to stop by his house to grab some clothes and check-in with Lisa. He didn't talk to her for over a week now, and feels nervous to whatever way she will welcome him in the flat.

After having breakfast together and Aaron carrying his search for getting a full picture of his last 24 hours. It is true that since they came back from the warehouse assault, a lot of work has been needed on the cars between the impact of the explosion of the car, the charge into the main gates and carrying over blooded bodies and lots of equipment. As well, lots of modification were needed to reverse all the changes done on the cart to accommodate the operation. Aaron suffered quite heavily of the loss of Diarmuid and he chose to bury himself into the garage's workload instead of sitting down and trying to process it in his head.

He went through the two days hanging on coffee and bread.

Now he gets min Erin's car as she drives him to his place

- How long do you think it's gonna take you two to discuss?

- Don't wait for me, I'll call the garage when I am ready to be picked up, they can send someone

- Okay, let me know how you get on.

Arriving at the building, turning the key into the entrance door to unlock it, he feels his blood racing in his veins, like he could feel his heart beating in his head. Walking up the stairs, the feeling in his head intensifies. Here he is, in front of the apartment's door. Big deep breathe. Selecting his key, putting it in the lock, but very quickly realising that the key wouldn't fit in. Then Aaron tries all the keys he has on his key ring, out of confusion. Nothing works. 'I can't believe it, she changed the lock'. No noise inside, neither voices or other sounds. He tries to reach out to Lisa on her mobile, no answer whatsoever. After the third try, he calls a fourth time and it goes straight into voicemail.

' I can see it's starting on a positive note, this is going to be fun.'He then calls the garage and Sean comes to pick him up. 'We are not going back to the garage, let's go for a spin' he says to Aaron when the latter opens the car door.

Sean takes the direction of the outskirts of the town, and finally parks nearby a park. 'Let's go for a walk, you look like shit, man'.

- Listen, I know Diarmuid passing away has hit you hard, he has always fondly looked after you and is partly responsible for who you are today. But when we sign for this organisation, we know what to expect, and death is just part of the overall picture. Diarmuid knew the risks, appreciated the balance between risks and rewards. You've got to move on from that in your head. Yes it is sad and we are all aching his death, but we all keep our head high and we keep moving, this organisation is at a tricky point of its history. We need all tho chip in and stick together, we cannot afford anyone to fall over.

- I … I see what you mean. It's hard, you know. It really is. I mean… he has always been around, I know I'm not there for as long as you arre, but he was there to teach me, to explain, to discuss, to listen. Who is going to do that now?

- All of us. Niall, Tom, Aiden, Lee, Ian, Liam, the Nomads, myself… you have to realise each and every one of us is never going to be as big as the organisation as a whole is.

- I know what you mean. I know I should pick myself up and dust myself off. I guess I just need to say goodbye to him this evening and then we will move on with our lives.

- Alright, let's do like this. I've put Ian and Liam at the garage, I'll drive you there but you don't need to work, just catch up with everyone, there are a couple of friends as well, you can have small talks.

- Small talks, exactly what I love to do, hey!

Walking back to the car, the two men exchange their views on the past few days, between the attacks, the deaths, the mercenaries, the warehouse, … so much happened in so little time. Finally making their way to the garage, they find it filled with people, arrived early for the wake in memory of Diarmuid.

Niall wanted it packed, it is packed.

Sean and Aaron walk through the crowd and make their way up to the clubhouse. Even more people in there, the atmosphere is suffocating. Sean turns around to Aaron and tells him to go to the meeting room.

Niall, Aiden, Tom and now Sean are sitting at the table, while Aaron closes the doors behind him.

- You couldn't find something better to wear?, says Tom.

- I couldn't get into my apartment, Lisa changed the locks…

- Ladies, huh… Anyway, we had an officers' meeting this morning, to discuss the plan going forward to replace Diarmuid. We didn't agree unanimously to it therefore we decided it was too early for you to step in for his role. You're very committed in anything Security-related, but you lack a bit of composure in your approach, it's all a bit too reckless at the moment. We will put Aiden to head the Security, you'll work for him and we will have Joe from the Nomads joining the team too. It's time we expand our operations especially with this nice new warehouse.

- We think you should stick to the garage for now, and there will be enough to do with the new jobs we've got lined up ahead of us, continues Tom. Aiden will supervise it all, you give your input and your energy, that should work for now.

- Are you saying it's never going to be on the table for me to be the Security Officer, or just not now, asks Aaron.

- Not now, son, just not now. Give yourself the time, finishes Niall.

Aaron nods his head in agreement and walks out of the room. The lounge area is really crowded, but he manages to make himself a way out of there towards the garage. Ian and Liam are finishing a car, the Nomads are smoking and drinking together. The garage door opens again, Erin walks in. While she is dressed all in black, just like every-one else around here, 'she really stands out', things Aaron. She walks confidently across the mass of people, saluting friends and family from the organisation. She finally makes it to reach Aaron:

- Hey..

- Hey, stranger. Thanks again for breakfast.

- that's not my favorite way to start the day but let's say it was okay for today.

She walks away after this cheeky comment and a wink. The garage door closes, and Sean walks out of the club-house 'Boys, it's time for the ceremony, get yourself up here'. The coffin is brought out of one of the bedrooms at the back of the clubhouse by the Nomads crew. Only few people can remember, but Diarmuid was sent up North to create the Nomads charter 10 years ago to recruit in the poorer areas, secluded from modern progress and incline to social inequalities. The coffin is then carried down to the garage, with Nomads singing their traditional songs and dropping it in the middle of the garage.

An Irish flag is lined on top of the coffin, and all members are circled around. After a couple of minutes of complete silence, Niall drops Diarmuid jacket on top and waves at the Nomads. They start their final song, which tells the story of a little boy moving from a countryside to the city to build his own life and ends up fighting for his own soul.

Once the men stop singing, the crowd slowly start moving towards the exit, to invade the sidewalks of the street. The garage and the clubhouse start settling in. The Nomads carry the coffin into their own van, and jump onboard. The rest of the organisation is standing in the garage now empty from all the guests. Erin walks back in from the street and grabs Aaron in her arms. Lee brings a plate with whisky shots.

'To Diarmuid Scott, great brother, great man, great friend, and a fantastic Security Officer. May you rest in Peace', solemnly says Niall before everyone down their shot.

'Boys, let's all take an hour or two for ourselves, then we are back to business.'

Everyone walks up the stairs to the clubhouse and find a spot on the couches and chairs. Erin cuddles Aaron, playing with his curly hair. A couple of dogs running around and Lee playing his guitar. It is good for everyone to have some quiet time, the last days having been so hectic. Aaron's phone is ringing, it's Lisa.

-   Hey, thanks for calling back.

-   Well, you remembered you had a son? And a girlfriend if that's still what I am to you?

-   Yeah, sorry, things have been really hectic around here. I got my cut this morning, wanted to come and drop it but I guess I need a new key to get into the flat I'm paying the rent for.

- I can see you're more worried about the money than you are worried about us.

- Well you don't let me worry about you, so I do with what I see. Now, we can carry on fighting over the phone or you let me come over and we can discuss in person? You know, like grown ups?

- Fine, I'm home now, you can come over, if you're not planning to kill or torture anyone today.

- Jesus, very funny. Alright I'm on my way.

He turns around to Erin without a word, smiles and walks out. Arriving at the residence, he decides to leave his jacket in the car. Making his way up the stairs, and knocking on the door. Hearing steps behind the door. Lock turning. Door handle dropping. Door opening.

'Get in', says Lisa. Aaron walks in and goes straight to the living room. Lisa didn't follow him, but soon turns up in the room with a coffee mug in her hand. The tension is palpable on her face.

- Drink this, you look like shit. When was the last time you slept?, she is asking.

- Where is Luke? I brought him a little something.

- He is at my mom's place. I didn't want him to hear us fighting… again. He knows something is wrong, but he keeps on asking about you and about when you will be back home.

- I … we… we just had a tough week at the garage, I worked around the clock.

- Do you really think I am THAT stupid? You don't think people talk around town?

- Wait.. what do you mean?

- Well now you're famous around town. Everyone got to know the new shining star of Rising Skulls. You walk around town with your jacket and your new friends like you own the place.

Aaron pulls a brown envelope from his bag and hands it over to her.

- What's this?, she asks.

- That's my cut for the past two weeks. It's five thousand euro. When was the last time we got that amount of cash in our hands?

- I don't want it, she says throwing the envelope to his face… that's dirty money!

- So you would rather starve to death with our kid rather than having that money?

- YES!, she continues, because that means I don't live on dirty money, or even worth.. did you kill someone to get that money?

- I didn't kill anyone... I fixed and prepared cars, and drove my car around with people at the back. Alive people.

They both go into silence, looking at each other. Lisa suddenly falls on a chair and starts crying. He stands there, petrified. He knew in the back of his head that what he was doing was not what she wanted, nor what she imagined her partner would be doing. But somehow, he was hoping she would end up accepting his choice when seeing the financial rewards of it. Clearly, she wasn't accepting any of it.

She still sits, she still cries. He still stands, he still stays silent. He finally decides to move towards her, but she raises her right arm towards him to stop him:

- Don't you dare. Don't touch me with these hands that must still be blood-stained.

- You can hate me for what I do, you can hate me for who I've become, he calmly tells her. But remember, I am still the father of our boy, and once upon a time you saw your future with me. Now I recommend you to think deep before pushing me away. You can run away, you can hide away, but you can't forget what we have been, what we should be and what we can still be.

She can't speak a word back to him. Lisa sees him walk out, while the brown envelops stays on the floor of the living room, while Aaron slams the door behind him as he leaves the apartment. Getting back to the garage, he goes directly to the team working on the last car and starts changing the exhaust line that got hit during the journey to the warehouse.

There is a big activity going on around the garage, Diarmuid's funerals being done now, everyone is back to normal life, at least what looks like normal life. Members are constantly in and out, dropping new cars to work on, back from protection jobs with local gang members that pay the Rising Skulls for protection during their own business meetings. Aiden is really working hard on developing the business, Niall keeps on bringing new members, Sean is setting up dummy corporations to cover for their other activities.

It's now two days since he spoke to Lisa and nothing, not a single message since then. He stays at the clubhouse more and more, or crashes occasionally at one of the member's house. It's good to keep himself busy, days go by fast and there are always someone around to talk to. Tom and Aiden have kept Aaron away from any operation to let him settle in after Diarmuid's death and make sure he is back on his feet.

Five days now have gone by, still no sign of Lisa. The No-mads are in town to take over the control of the new ware-house, and they stopped by the garage to grab some equip-ment and get a few members to join them. Lots of noise in the garage when Aaron hears Lee, who is at the gate, shout 'There is a girl here, not sure who she is. Can someone come?'. Aarom starts running towards the gate when it opens up and he sees Lisa standing there, with Luke next to her.

The little boy runs towards his dad, with his mother walk-ing slowly behind him. Aaron grabs him in his arms and lifts him up.

- Hey little man, it's good to see you, I missed you.

- Daddy. What happened? Why did you disappear?

- You know, son, daddy had to travel for his work, I had a lot of cars to fix. But now I am back, I am here.

- Aaron, please, don't give me false hopes, inter-venes Lisa.

- Alright son, daddy needs to talk to mommy, can you go play over there for a minute?

Both parents stand still as their little one runs to the corner of the garage and start playing with a ball against the wall. Aaron looks at his girlfriend and says:

\- When was the last time we both looked at him playing?

\- Too long. Aaron, he needs a father, you know he loves you, he loves spending time looking at you working. Please do something.

\- And you, Lisa, do you love me? Do you love spending time with me as well?

\- I … I don't know. For me it's not the same. It's not like before, I am sure you can understand that. But for him, he is only a little boy. He doesn't deserve to suffer from your choices.

\- My choices? Just grow up, just fucking grow up. We were just crashing completely into poverty and he would have had to face that we were not able to feed ourselves anymore. So as far as I'm concerned, I did what I had to do. If you're thinking otherwise, you're just kidding yourself, finishes Aaron as he walks towards his son.

The garage gate opens up, and it is Erin walking in. Looking up and down on Lisa, she walks straight to Aaron and kneels down to play with Aaron and Luke. The father picks his son in his arms again, with Erin grabbing his toy and shaking it in front of the kid's face to play with him. Lisa's face turns to red as she walks right between Aaron and Erin to grab Luke off his dad's arms.

- Come here, Luke, let's get you something to eat.

- Oh well, look who turns up once every month and wants to rule the place, follows Erin.

- Erin, please, don't start, answers Aaron.

As Lisa walks away with her son in her arms, she looks back to show her discontent to Niall's daughter. He walks behind her and walks her to the clubhouse. On the way up, the Nomads are approaching her. She walks away at first holding her son even tighter. Aaron stops her, and asks her to give him Luke. He then grabs and settles his kid in his arms, and walks to the Nomads, with Lisa following him closely and saying 'we shouldn't expose him to these people'. Aaron gets within the Nomads' pack and Jerry gets closer:

- Is that your son, Aaron?

- Yes, Jerry, this is Luke. And this is Lisa, my girl-friend.

- Lisa, very nice to meet you, I'm Jerry. This is Stephen, Joe and the shy one there is Matt, continues Jerry as he turns to speak directly to Lisa with a big smile on his face.

- Hmm, hello Jerry, .. eh, likewise, as she shakes his hand very timidly.

- If you need anything, you can always ask me or my guys. Aaron's girlfriend is a Nomads' friend, continues Jerry.

As Aaron realises Lisa's surprise is more than total, he grabs her by the shoulder and shows her the direction to the clubhouse, while looking back and winking at the Director. Clearly, she didn't expect them too be friendly, she probably didn't even expect them to be human. He sets them in on one of the couches, and brings water for the boy and coffee for the girlfriend. The clubhouse is unexpectedly calm, with the radio playing at the back.

- Where is everyone? I was expecting this place to be much more busy, asks Lisa.

- Niall and Sean are visiting a customer, Tom and Aiden are supervising the repair work we do to a warehouse up North, Lee, Ian and Liam are doing some runs for customers. The Nomads are here to pick up some material and tools for the warehouse so they will soon be leaving too.

- Wow... well when you say it like this, it just sounds like a normal business.

- Babe, listen. I know you don't like it, and I don't question that. But if you would keep your mind open just a little, you would realise this is not as bad as you think. I'm not asking you to look the other way, I'm not asking you to close your eyes.

I'm asking you to keep your eyes open and give it a chance. After a fair try, if you still don't like it, I'll cash out and leave, I promise you. I want our boy to grow up with a dad, but as well with a nice comfortable home with enough food for everyone every day of the month and every month of the year. Give me the chance to provide that and we can work something out.

- I must say I'm confused right now, Aaron. Give me some time and let me get my head around being with you in this whole thing.

- Take all the time you want, I support that you do so. So, I've got to go and finish the car downstairs, when you're done with feeding our boy, just pop back down.

Lisa just looks around and she still can't believe how 'normal' this feels like. Just like a normal garage with cars in and out the whole day. A while after that, Lisa comes down alone:

- Where is Luke? Is everything okay?

- Yes, he is sleeping on the couch.

Lisa is sitting on the metallic stairs while looking at her boyfriend working on the car. He puts the wheels back on, checks the chassis, refills tanks of oil and windscreen washer, checks the front lights projection levels.

'All set, let me get this car turned around' as he jumps into it. He then walks back to her and sits next to her.

They keep on talking, with some of the old feelings of complicity coming back little by little.

Suddenly, the gate opens and one of the Skulls' SUV rushes inside. Lee and Ian walk out of the front doors.

- What's going on, boys?, screams Joe running towards the car.

- It's Liam, he got shot in the shoulder, it's really bad, answers Lee.

- Ok, let's bring him upstairs, shouts Aaron, as he runs up to open the door and prepare the room.

Lisa stands there just looking around her, people running, then Liam's body carried up the stairs completely covered in blood. What seemed like a normal working place until two minutes ago now definitely looks like a war zone. She can't move, nor can she think. A minute later, Aaron flies down the stairs with their son in his arms, and her bag, and says:

- Here, grab him, I've got to go and help patching him up. I'll call you later.

- I guess our honeymoon is already over, isn't it?, answers Lisa.

- Daddy, what's going on? Why is the man over there screaming?, is asking the little boy.

- He did a mistake when he was working, he used some tools without paying attention and he injured himself. That's a good reminder that you shouldn't touch any of daddy's tools or all the dangerous things a home like knifes and electric tools. You understand what I mean, son?

- Yes, daddy.

Aaron kisses both his son and his girlfriend and walks back to the clubhouse.

'It feels good to be close to them again.', he thinks, as he sees them leaving the garage. It is definitely a moment like this that wakes something up in his guts, something about the good and bad, the joy of family life and the responsibility he has towards his child growing up looking at him.

Chapter 8: Ascencio

The Rising Skulls organisation really got into a routine, the warehouse now opening to high-security storage run by the Nomads, and the rest of the business handled by Niall and his crew. Little by little, Aaron is getting more and more duties around Security, which started including customer meetings alongside Niall or Tom. Lisa agreed to start coming once a week so Luke could play with his dad and could see what his dad is up to. Aaron started coming back home more often and sometimes go home early to pick his son up at work. But the looks on people's faces when they would see Aaron walking out of his car sometimes still wearing his Skulls jacket. Some people would look at him with respect and appreciation, some others like he had the plague.

Having found that balance between his family life and his work life made him feel more emotionally stable and both Niall and Aiden have noticed his development. And they still have not made their decision for promoting Aaron as Security Officer. But they know it is time to put Aaron through his last test.

Aaron is on the road with Ian to collect some cargo destined for storage at the warehouse, when he gets a call on his mobile from Tom. He doesn't pick up and tells Ian:

- We are two minutes away from the customer, I'll call him back after loading.

- And I guess he doesn't want to wait, he is calling me now, follows quickly Ian after a few seconds.

Aaron parks the car in front of the office part of the warehouse, while Ian stays on the phone with Tom.

'No need to get out of the car, Tom needs you back at the garage.', finishes Ian as he steps out of the car.

On the way back to the garage, he tries guessing what this is all about. Did he do something wrong? At the garage, or with customers? Did he give the wrong information about something? It's a long journey back for him and his heart rate just keeps increasing as he gets closer to destination. 5 more minutes and here he is, with Lee opening the gate for him. He drives inside and stops at his usual spot. No one in the garage, so he walks up the stairs to the clubhouse. The meeting room doors are open, with both the Director and the Operations Manager sitting at the table. Aaron walks in the room:

- You wanted to see me? I'm here.

- Sit down, Aaron, answers Niall, as Aaron moves towards the end of the table, where he usually sits.

- No, sit down here, follows Niall pointing out to the seat where Diarmuid used to sit.

- But… it's Diarmuid's seat. I mean, it's the Security Officer seat.

- If you make me tell you a third time, I break your legs, kid.

Aaron sits down.

- Do you like this seat?

- Of course, you know I would love to take that promotion.

- Well, Aaron, today is the day we start your last test. If you pass, you get the job, if you fail, we put Aiden there. Sounds fair enough?

- Aye. What do you need me to do?

- Well Aaron, intervenes Tom, we have that big new prospect. They handle all kind of car and bike spare parts , repack and distribute. However, their current logistics provider is… well.. they got busted by the police. Looks like they got infiltrated for a few months and then got caught receiving a huge shipment inbound. We need you to meet the customer, talk them through what we can do, understand if and how many people we need to have to run their operation. We need to see as well what pricing model they had with the previous group, and how they want it to be in the future. Niall and myself have already spoken to them, they heard of us and somehow managed to know about our new warehouse project with the Nomads.

- I guess this could be a good way to maximise the warehouse. When is the meeting planned?

- First thing in the morning. We have other meetings so you will have to go with someone else alongside you. We already gave your name to them as they wanted to run a background check.

- I'll check in with the Nomads, I think it would make sense if they are part of it, as they will run the place and whatever activity we put in it.

- Great idea, says Niall. Here is the address and the contact name. 10AM tomorrow. Don't be late - he finishes, handing over a sticky note to Aaron.

Aaron gets back in the car ... to drive back to the warehouse - 'I'll end up driving up and down with my eyes closed'. He wants to get a run through of the warehouse operations with the Nomads.

After an hour on site, looking at the different loading bays, review all access roads, the surrounding fences, the CCTV system, he is ready to go back home and get refreshed because the big meeting of the next day.

It's 18:30 when he arrives home, as Lisa is giving bath to Luke. He stands by the door of the bathroom just watching his girlfriend and their son, having a moment together, playing candidly.

'After all, being part of a gang and having a family life aren't two contradictory things.', he thought at that time.

Maybe that's all he needed. Some time to find the balance, to make efforts for both work and family without jeopardising one or the other. Having dinner with Lisa gives him the chance to switch off from all the tension linked with his activities, just to be able to listen to her life, her funny stories, her frustrations and her achievements. To have some innocent moments together, just like at the beginning of their relationship, when they had no money problem, no pressure, nothing to worry about, just two people that love each other very much and are just enjoying each other's company.

Dropping Luke at the kindergarten is one of these things that Aaron didn't do in months, but feeling like it was years ago since last time he kissed his head and wished him to have a good day.

Quick check-in at the garage, then on his way to the meeting location with Joe on the passenger seat. Arriving on site, there is a very impressive presence of people from the prospect customer. As soon as the two members step out of the car, a few men walk towards them, hands on guns.

- Is it really necessary, asks Aaron as he gets searched for. In my back, Berettta 9 millimetres.

- It's just a precaution, gentlemen, I am sure you can understand, answers one of the men in suits.

- Aaron Salerini, good to meet you. This is Joe Malone, a colleague of mine.

- Pete Ross, and this is my associate Michael Poulsen. Let's discuss in our office, shall we?, he says showing a shipping container dropped in a corner.

- I can see you've chosen a glamorous office location, finishes Aaron as they walk behind their hosts.

Inside the container, two desks, and a proper meeting table surrounded by chairs. Pete, Michael, Aaron and Joe sit down at the table:

- Before I start, Joe and myself would like to thank you for inviting us to discuss this opportunity, on behalf of the Rising Skulls organisation.

- Good, continues Pete. Now let us explain you what we need.

Follows a detailed explanation of the goods supply routings, security requirements, dispatch methods, potential risk areas. This is clearly a huge project. And there will need to be investments made into the warehouse, especially for the security levels required.

- What I think we could do, is to create a caged area in a corner of the warehouse, with dedicated loading bays that we can upgrade for the locking systems as well. Separate CCTV system that we can grant you live access to. But this won't come within a day and there is a decent price tag associated with the investment.

- We can cover the investment 'like for like', that's no problem. But we will supply the manpower.

- I'm afraid not. We run the operations, we run the manpower. You can have access to them directly, but we manage them, continues Aaron.

- I'm not feeling great about external manpower handling our business but …

- But you are feeling great about external company providing a roof to your cargo, I guess..

- Alright, you got a point, kid. We let you go back to your organisation and you let us know by the end of the week how much it's going to cost to set us up and by when do you plan to be operational. We've got to handle the handover with the current temporary solution we have put in place.

Everyone shake hands and Aaron and Joe get on their way to go back to the garage. The debrief with Niall and Tom happens very quickly and Aaron is sent home, 'Tomorrow is a big day, you've got a lot to figure out for this project' said Niall.

The next couple of days, Aaron and Joe are fringing different steal suppliers, CCTV companies, going to local DIY shops for locks and other equipments. The real challenge when you do something illegal, is that you will have to do everything by yourself.

'How to explain them that by doing their job, they help us sett up an illegal business?', laughed Aaron to Joe when they were cold calling suppliers.

Little by little, they manage to tackle all the aspects, but there will be a big need for manual effort to install everything in a short timeframe.

Time for a debrief with the boss:

- We could get supply of all material needed, within the next 5 to 6 working days. Including CCTV systems, all the new locks, the metallic cage and the other bits and pieces. But to get it all installed and ready for go-live, we will need all the manpower we need. This is really heavy work.

- We have so many runs lined up for the next couple of weeks, says Tom, this will be hard to free up anyone aside of the Nomads...

- Then I guess it will be a very busy couple of weeks.

They then discuss the pricing model that the potential customer has wished for, and all the other details, as well as the access to funds to pay upfront the materials.

Jerry and Joe managed to get a few 'friends' to help with the warehouse upgrades and the work starts a couple of days later. A few technical issues later, it start taking shape and within a week, all security features are set. The high ceiling of the warehouse makes the installation of the security cage. A bit more than a third of the warehouse is turned into a dedicated area for inbound, storage, picking, packing and outbound shipping to all consignees, mostly to local car dealers and private garages.

On the last day of the installation, Aaron invites the customer to come over, visit the facility, validate that they are happy with the setup and paying for all the invoices.

It's a big day for the Rising Skulls, and a proud one for sure for Aaron as he is finishing the design of his first big project. The convoy of cars from the customer arrives late afternoon, as the entire Rising Skulls crew stands in front of the warehouse, making an impression from the outset. The guests step out of the car, and Niall walks towards them:

- Welcome gentlemen, it's a pleasure to have you joining us.

- Hi Niall, good to see you again, follows Michael. We are looking forward to see what you guys prepared for us.

- Aaron will walk you through the whole setup, he has been our Project Manager for this as you know, he will give you all the details you want to know, continues Niall as he points out towards Aaron.

- Gentlemen, good to see you again. Welcome to Rising Park, our very own warehouse. Our fencing is equipped with motion detector in case someone is trying to slice it open. Full CCTV coverage from the outside, with cameras protected from any shooting with any standard firearm.

- Very impressive, says Pete.

- Now, let's step inside and we can continue the tour, continues Aaron.

The presentation continues inside, with the guests being more and more impressed by the technical setup and the operational capacities of the Rising Skulls. Aaron is really proudly showing them around 'his' warehouse.

After over an hour of detailed review of all the installations, the management of both organisations walk into the meeting room.

- So, opens Niall, your impressions?

- Clearly, you guys have taken us very seriously, answers Pete. You have listened to our requirements and expectations. I think you tick all the boxes and I must say we are very impressed by how fast this was all done. So, we would like to proceed further.

- Good, very good, continues Niall. Aaron, can you provide the invoices please?

- So here we are. All invoices as requested, all the material like new locks, CCTV, security cage, remote connectivity, fencing sensors. For a grand total of eighty-seven thousand euro, all on invoices. The warehouse racking and the consumables are on us.

- And to finish on the commercial offering, we propose you to charge a flat fee for the usage of the warehouse, so more you use and better it is for you. For the delivery fees, we already discussed last time about fix fee per destination.

- I must admit I find this very expensive for the setup costs, I'm okay with the rest. But if I compare with the set costs we have paid to our current partner, it's almost double.

- We will let you discuss internally, we are outside whenever you are ready, says Niall as he gets up from his chair and touches Tom's arm to signal him to stand up too.

- I understand your nervousness, you know, says Aaron who is still sitting. I get it, new partner, lots of money on the table, new ways of working, and so on. But before you try to save a few dozen thousands euro, let me remind you that you came to us, not the other way around. I'm pretty sure your current provider might be cheaper but must be shit. So see it as an investment into your future profit that will be made possible only because we will run the best operations you can hope for.

Aaron finally stands up, smiles at his two hosts and follows Niall and Tom outside the meeting room.

'That was very well done, Aaron, no matter what happens, you've done a great job.' Says Niall before showing him to move away.

It's only after half an hour that the meeting room door opens to see Michael walking out and say 'We're ready' to Niall and Tom. Aaron is still working wit the Nomads, supervising the finishing touches of the security cage and the storage racks. He gets called in by Tom.

The three members of the Skulls settle back in the meeting room. The tension is palpable around the table. If the customer doesn't make a deal with them, that's all the investments done for nothing.

- We called our shareholders, starts Pete, to debrief them on the situation and the solution you guys have designed. And ... they agreed. They will unlock the cash for us and by early next week we will proceed with the payout of the setup costs.

- This is.. great news, answers Niall As you see, we are basically ready, so we will be able to receive the first shipment as soon as you've made the payment.

- Well, that's the point we have to discuss, continues Michael. We have a bit of a situation, and we would like our new partners to help us out. We have a very important shipment and no place to store it, our current partners are full and we see that your facility is up to the standards we require.

- And exactly by when do you exactly expect us to receive that shipment?

- Well, they told us it was already transhipped in Liverpool, will take the ferry tonight in Holyhead be there tomorrow lunch time.

Niall and Tom turn around straight away to Aaron, which nods his head in silence to confirm his setup is fully finished and ready to go.

- It's not ideal but we will make it work, confirms Niall. Just send us the details of the cargo and who should we expect and the ETA of the cargo. Aaron will make sure this goes successfully.

- For sure, we keep you posted, finishes Pete as he gets up, shakes hands with Niall and walks out alongside Michael.

Aaron cannot hide his joy on his face. Tom taps on his shoulder and walks out too. Niall is sitting, looking at him. Aaron doesn't understand why he is not saying anything at all. The boss gets up, slowly walks towards him. Aaron gets up too. 'Congratulations on this great deal, Security Officer'. He is speechless. Niall now walks out. Aaron falls back on his chair, a huge smile on his face, eyes closed. Savouring the moment he worked towards for some time now. He is an officer of the Rising Skulls. What a moment.

But not much of a time for celebration as Joe is smashing open the door of the meeting room, asking Aaron to confirm if they are really receiving a shipment tomorrow morning.

A few things to finish off, the on-site presence to plan, to ensure the right amount of people are ready without impacting the rest of the business. A last few practical arrangements with the security cage and a final round of CCTV checks, at around 10 o'clock at night, Aaron finally leaves the site confident everything is now ready for the first delivery.

His sleep rather agitated and short, the new Security Officer gets up early and decides to check in early at the garage to get all the equipments needed at the warehouse. He kisses Lisa's head as she is still asleep, then does the same to his little boy before walking out in silence. After a quick stop at the garage, he makes his way to the warehouse, where he arrives to find Nomads already presents and strongly armed. The gate opens and he drives through. Time for the last preparations.

The Nomads crew got a few new faces in the last couple of weeks, to help with the running of the warehouse activities. 'We must not have been doing much of a background check on them', thinks Aaron as he enters the warehouse.

Full walk-through of the inbound and storage processes, review of roles for everyone involved, and final check of the locks. Meanwhile, Aaron has tasked few of the Nomads to start cutting down the closest trees from the fencing, so the security team can see people walking out of the woods from further away.

By lunch time, all the preparations are finalised, every single aspect of the warehouse has been looked gatt and checked twice and every team member has been briefed, probably twice too.

Aaron's mobile phone rings. It's Niall:

- Aye, boss?

- Aaron, just got a call from Pete, the truck has ETA 14:30, registration plate 162-D-19634. I'll send you as many members as possible.

- We already have an army here, but I'll take anyone you want to land me.

- Make me proud, Aaron. Don't fuck this one up.

Just before the planned ETA of the truck, Aiden arrives on site. 'Everything is ready, let's grab a coffee and wait for them'.

It's only few minutes later that the truck arrives. The two security guards stop the truck, check the truck number, then let it through, opening the main gate. Pressure on all the members' faces, hands on their guns. The driver and his passenger get off their truck cabin and walk towards Aaron and Aiden. 'Gate number 3', shouts Aaron towards them.

The truck manoeuvres around and tips to the gate. Aaron is the first one to walk towards the opened trailer. Big metal crates on pallets, with no sign nor indication on the outside to whatever is inside.

The driver walks quickly inside to look at the handling of the cargo.

- Do you guys know when will this be dispatched, asks Aaron.

- That's not our business, mate, we are only here to deliver and get out of here.

- The crates are locked, do yo have the keys?

- Do I look like I have keys to crates?, finishes the driver before stepping out of Joe arrives at full speed with the forklift.

Within 15 minutes, the truck is emptied and sent on its way. The three metal crate are put into the secured cage area, and Aaron locks everything himself as he leaves the storage area. After a quick call to Niall to confirm that everything went well, there is a huge noise in the background:

- What's going on, Niall, where are you?

- The police raided the garage, they are turning everything upside down, we can't be leaving the place. They are raiding all our houses and they are going to our families and friends as well.

- Gold Almighty, okay I'll call Lisa.

After a few tries, he still can't get any answer from her. So he jumps in his car and drives straight back home, putting his car to its limit across the countryside roads.

As he arrives around the last corner, he doesn't see any police Carr or any sign of unusual activity. But no sign of Lisa either. He decides then to go to her workplace. Not there either. 'Third time is a charm', he thinks, as he drives to Luke's kindergarten. Within minutes, he gets there. Here she is, walking out of the kindergarten carrying their son in her arms:

- Lisa, over here, he shouts, as he jumps out of his car.

- Hey babe, good to see you, what's going on? I thought you were busy at work today?

- Yes I was, but we have had a situation, the police is raiding the garage and turning up at all our families' houses for interrogation.

- What's going on? Why are they doing this?

- If only I knew why... Let me drive you to our secured warehouse, it's safe there and no one knows yet we are based there as well.

- But Aaron, why? Why hiding?

- Because I don't know what they want from you, and I don't want to take any risk.

- What risks? What would happen to us?

- I prefer not to find out and to bring you to the warehouse until we know more. Give me your Carr keys, I'll grab your baby seat and fit it in my car.

Within a couple of minutes, the baby seat is fitted, Luke is strapped in, Aaron and Lisa sitting at the front ready to go. He puts his hand on hers and tells her 'I won't let anything happen to you, I swear', as he sees the panic settle on her face.

Within 40 minutes he arrives at the warehouse, and his girlfriend isn't short of panic seeing all the Nomads carrying automatic weapons and bulletproof vests. He gets his little family settled in the meeting room, with tea and water, then asks Lisa:

- What else do you need?

- Well, I didn't pack any food especially for him.

- Ok I'll send someone to grab food. Wait here, okay? I'll check in as soon as I can.

Aaron then disappears into the warehouse. He calls Niall back, without success. Same outcome with Tom, Sean and Ian. He sees Lee is just arriving in front of the entrance of the compound.

He stops him, opens the passenger door, jumps in the car and tells him to drive back out. 'We need to stock up on food, we will lock everything down'.

After several trials, he still can't reach out to anyone. Meant to be at the garage. They manage to find a grocery shop a few kilometres down the road in a small countryside town.

Within minutes, they are back at the warehouse, dropping all the groceries in the meeting room. 'Alright take care of our boy, I'll try to find out more about what's going on'.

Followed by Lee and Stephen, Aaron walks out of the warehouse and sees a grey Ford Focus at the gate, with the security guards talking to its passengers.

- What's this car doing here? No one knows we are here, says the Security Officer.

- We had no one else scheduled for today, confirms Stephen.

- Guns out, boys.

As the three of them are advancing slowly towards the security gate, Lee notices something moving on the opposite side of the compound.

'AARON, POLICE OVER THERE', he shouts, as he points out the corner of the compound showing people coming out of the forest in large number.

Stephen calls on the radio for backup and everyone comes out of the warehouse, all weapons out. There is approx hundred meters between where they stand and where the intruders are now looking like they are attacking the fence with a cutting saw. Sparks are flying everywhere.

'EVERYONE, GET INSIDE!'

They all rush into the meeting room to open the locked cabinet where a reserve of riffles are stored. Lisa and Luke are scared to death with all of this.

- Aaron, what's going on again?

- Police is there, they are assaulting the compound, we will defend this place, don't worry, everything will be okay.

They all walk out with weapons and rounds of ammunition. The squad they now make is moving towards the emergency exit door right at the corner of the warehouse. But what they find in front of them when opening the door is much more than just a few men. Dozens of them. With enough weapons in their hands to make a whole wall of the warehouse collapse. Aaron shuts the door back and turns to his squad:

- We won't get all out alive, there are too many of them.

- What are you saying then, boss, we surrender?, continues Stephen.

- We are Rising Skulls, we don't surrender to Police. People always trust us to stand to whoever is on the way to having a fair society, not being ran by corrupt politicians. It is our duty to fight these people that come to our families, to our friends, to get all of us behind bars for no valid reason.

- Gentlemen, I guess we are all clear on what we are about to do, says Lee. Let's avoid dramatic moments and let's get into it, shall we?

- Aim well, save your ammo, be brave, finishes Aaron as he loads his rifle, two hand guns slid into the back of his trousers. Let's go boys!

Everyone takes position around the doors, knowing that the Police forces will have to enter through them at some stage. Now the entire warehouse is in complete silence. From far away, the Security Officer can hear his son crying knowing that his girlfriend is in there completely panicked and it is his fault somehow. A deep breathe later, the conclusion being ' I can't make this not happening, but I can protect them from anyone else', he focuses on the doors. By now, Stephen, Lee, Joe, and the two Nomads that were at the security gate, that managed to go inside the building before being shot by the car passengers that presented itself causing distraction.

The silence remains. The tension within the group just keeps increasing, Aaron instructs the team to follow him on the first corner, towards the door closest to the compound entrance secured gates.

'Let's neutralise that team first, then we can take care of the bigger crowd'.

Joe opens the door slowly, with Stephen and Aaron ready to shoot right behind him. Suddenly, a grenade rolls up the stairs towards the inside. 'GET BAAACK', screams Joe as he kicks it back out, the grenade exploding in the stairs. Joe angrily rushes out to find the two policemen agonising.

Aaron runs out behind him, grabs him by the jacket to bring him back in, closing the door behind him.

- How about we use this door to extract Lisa and my boy if the rest of the police force is on the far end of the compound?

- Aaron, we need to keep everyone here, it's safer inside, continues Joe.

- I volunteer for that, staying here waiting to have everyone executed, while I could be trying my best to save a child and a woman, that's really not a choice for me, that's a must do, follows Stephen.

- I would do it myself but I have a responsibility here, to fight for the greater good, answers Aaron.

He then proceeds to run towards the meeting room, grab his girlfriend and their son and come back to the team.

- So what we do ... Stephen, you take them to my car, it's the closest one from this door straight on your left. At the same time, we will open the other door and fire as hard as possible to keep them focused on us. Send me a message when you're arrived somewhere safe. (Turning to Lisa) Don't worry babe, it's all gonna be okay. I'll see you two very soon.

He kisses them both on the forehead, and taps Stephen on the shoulder to make him move. Everyone gets on the move, they have to now create a diversion. Lisa looks at her boyfriend one last time as he runs ahead of his squad. Aaron whistles when they arrive the door so Stephen knows he can get ready to walk out.

'For the Rising Skulls, for our families, let's do this!', shouts Aaron as he opens the door. Joe jumps on the right side of the door and they both start shooting blindly. Soon their magazines are empty and Lee and the two Nomads take over. As Aaron and Jo step aside to reload, the Security Officer just hears Lee shout 'SHIIII-' and an explosion shakes Aaron's boy to send it against a pallet few meters away from where he was.

His vision is blurry, his breathing struggling, his hands shaking. When he finally manage to look up, all he can see is flames and the bodies of Lee and the Two Nomads on the floor, deceased.

Still seeing all blurry, he sees several silhouettes walking in the warehouse. His hands still shaking are looking for his gun, but a man is now standing in front of him, handgun pointed at his head. Blood dripping out of his mouth and his nose, the man looking down at him pushing his gun away:

- You really thought you could get away from the law, didn't you?, says the policeman.

- We ... we are the Rising Skulls, answers Aaron, we are the law.

The man gets closer to him, kneels down next to Aaron's face, his hand firmly in his hand. A shot is fired.

Printed in Great Britain
by Amazon